Growing Dread:

Biopunk Visions

Timid Pirate Publishing

C. Dombrowski, Editor

Direct all orders to:
Timid Pirate Publishing
509 N. 85th St. #14,
Seattle, WA 98103

www.timidpirate.com

ISBN 978-0-9830987-4-4
Printed in the United States of America
Timid Pirate Publishing: March, 2011

All characters in this book are fictitious. Any resemblance to actual scientists or vampires, living or dead, is purely coincidental.

Table of Contents

By Lea Barozzi

Introduction

Staring into the mossy eyes of a dark night, sipping our kombucha and listening to the howl of leaves against the sky, we at Timid Pirate gave screaming, nascent birth to the notion of a biology-based punk anthology... Like Victor Frankenstein before us, how could we have possibly known what our creation would become?

We invite you to crawl between these soft pages to discover these living tales; visions of utopia or prisons of the flesh, depending on how your brain interprets the signals. Bear witness to eleven visions of possible futures, warnings of dangers and hilarious consequences to envisioning biopunk.

We dedicate this to all those mad brewers, scientists and fermentation fiends. May your cultures prosper.

C. Dombrowski

We reject the popular perception that science is only done in million-dollar university, government, or corporate labs; we assert that the right of freedom of inquiry, to do research and pursue understanding under one's own direction, is as fundamental a right as that of free speech or freedom of religion.

A Biopunk Manifesto, Meredith Patterson

The First
Growth Cycle

Let both sides seek to invoke the wonders of
science instead of its terrors.
JFK

Muffin Everlasting
By Minerva Zimmerman

"There is something fascinating about science.
One gets such wholesale returns of conjecture out
of such a trifling investment of fact."
Mark Twain, *Life on the Mississippi*, 1883

I'm Synergy Creatures' go-to guy for impossible things.
My bosses automatically clear my workload every time the
owner's mouth-breathing son, Will, gets quoted in the industry
press. Will's normal pick-up routine involves bragging about
creatures under development no one in R&D has ever
hallucinated—much less tried to cobble together a prototype.
That's saying something. Mandatory drug testing would wipe out
the entire department.

I've managed to get Synergy's nuts out of the fire twice
before. The basilisk wasn't even particularly hard. Giant movie
serpents not withstanding, turns out no one is entirely certain
what basilisks are supposed to look like. I just slapped some
chicken and reptile DNA around until I got a half dozen viable
embryos that all looked roughly the same. The gryphon was a
bitch. Thanks to goddamn Harry Potter everyone and their
mother knows what those look like and weren't going to accept
whatever mixed bag of lion and eagle parts came up naturally.
Neither avian nor mammal DNA wanted to play nice with a total
of six limbs. Splicing in the limb sequences from grasshopper
DNA caused new issues. The first batch of prototypes after
adding that was horrifying. After nine years of splicing
prototypes—I don't horrify easily. Normally, my projects have

about forty rounds of non-viable prototypes and five or six viable ones. The Gryphon Project had seven hundred and four non-viable prototypes and thirty-nine viable ones. It took me seven prototypes just to select out all the stray ass-feathers the later ones sprouted at first molt.

Project Rainbow makes the Gryphon Project look like a walk in the park. Synergy Creatures needs a unicorn. Not just any unicorn—that's already been done by several of our competitors—a miniature unicorn suitable as a child's pet. Will managed to get quoted saying Synergy's miniature unicorn was designed without a digestive tract and got all of its nutrients from specially-engineered lumps of sugar. By the grace of the Flying Spaghetti Monster, Will's company-appointed minder managed to forcibly extricate him before he said it vomited rainbows and smelled like homemade cookies.

I like my hallucinogens as much as the next microbiologist, and I have some pretty whacked ideas in a folder labeled "impractical and in-executable" but I've never designed a creature without a digestive system. I spent four days thinking about quitting my job and finding a company that would support an extended tropical vacation while I waited out the two years of my non-compete clause. I'm not famous in conventional circles, but people who know the name Cameron Tarlow would stab their own mother to have me work for them. A pair of Synergy Creatures Gryphons costs more than a square block of New York real estate and, being the latest billionaire craze, sells as fast as the company can replicate them. Keeping gryphons requires a specialized enclosure (made by Synergy Creatures), a full-time Synergy Creatures trained zoologist, and Synergy Creatures proprietary gryphon food blend at a rate of forty pounds, per gryphon, per day. Like all Synergy Creatures products they're genderless, sterile, trademarked and copyrighted. Rule #1 of making genetically modified organisms: make sure you control the only means of propagation. Made by special order or not at all.

The more I thought about digestive systems, the less possible Project Rainbow seemed. I turned on my out-of-office message, hopped a plane for Sedona and spent the better part of two weeks chemically altered in a hotel room covered in Lisa Frank unicorn posters for inspiration. None came, but I somehow lost three pounds while eating mostly marshmallows.

I threw out the posters, ate a 20-ounce porterhouse steak, drank four detox smoothies and drove back to the airport for a redeye back to Philly. Somewhere over Missouri I woke up from a dream about tardigrades. Tardigrades, or water bears, are hardy microscopic animals that look a little like a cross between a caterpillar and a manatee. They can survive extreme temperatures, high pressure, dehydration, and even the vacuum of space. Water bears have an almost mythical reputation among the biologists who know and love them. While water bears still have digestive systems, there are certain species that only defecate when they molt, leaving feces behind in the shed skin. It was the perfect solution to my digestion conundrum.

I drove straight to the lab from the airport and caught my section's administrative assistant watching MTV's "16 and Pregnant" on the computer as I breezed into the office. I tried to shake the image out of my head as I opened the door to my laboratory. I really didn't need to know that about him.

"Igor, get me the genome sequence for every known species of tardigrades that defecates only upon molting." I pointed at the two interns sitting across the room. "TweedleDeb and TweedleDave, you're taking over everything he was working on."

My assistant sighed. "My name is Ingvar."

I rolled my eyes. Of course I KNEW that. You'd think he'd have a sense of humor about it by now.

Ingvar canceled his dinner date and emailed me the sequences before I got to my third cup of coffee. I used the whiteboard to graph how well they'd play with other species' DNA. After the gryphon project, I've got a pretty good idea of how things do and don't work in poly-species splicing. I quickly narrowed down the choices to five different species, closed my eyes and picked one at random via rubber-dart-gun. With that out of the way, I looked for the other animal sequences. Narwal was pretty obvious, but I didn't want to use any of the existent varieties of miniature horse. I selected sequences from five different species of standard sized horses and added albinism. Since I cobbled the horse parts, it made sense to use the water bear genome as the base for the chimera. Instead of adding miniaturization to a horse genome, I spliced gigantism into the water bear. It was easier to tell the water bear-chimera to look like a horned horse than it was to tell a horse-chimera to digest and molt like a water bear. On a whim I added peacock iridescence into the chimera's chitin information. What the hell.

Ingvar and I both checked the chimera's assembled genome for obvious errors. After switching off some less desirable traits and removing a few conflicts in the code, I sent it to the Animal Genome Database Splicer we commonly refer to as the FrankenBox. It works like a little like genetic print-on-demand. The guy who invented it was classmate of mine at MIT. Bastard owns his own island now.

"All of the short-term vials in the Synthwomb Array are already in use." Ingvar rubbed at his eyes in sleep-deprived frustration.

I looked over his shoulder at the remote access screen. "Use one of the five liter full-term ones."

Ingvar keyed in the instructions and then turned control of the keyboard over to me. I entered my employee code to override the system block on full-term vials for first-time prototypes. The computer accepted my code, I loaded the vial with a modified egg, set it for 'expedited gestation' and we both went home to sleep.

Eighteen hours and All You Can Eat Pancakes later, I pulled up the vial's history to see when and how the prototype had lost viability. It hadn't.

"Ingvar..." I pointed at the screen. My mouth opening and closing as I struggled for words.

The lanky Swede practically sprinted across the lab.

Ingvar frowned at the computer and immediately called the help desk. There were no known problems with any systems this morning. TweedleDeb was dispatched to physically verify the information at the Array console. No one gets a viable prototype of any kind on the first go. It just doesn't happen.

While I was repeating this to myself as a skeptic's mantra,

my computer beeped and flashed up a dialog window: Gestation Complete.

I secured the vial for "manual harvest only" and sprinted across the industrial complex to the Gestation Lab. I scrubbed down and suited up to enter the clean lab faster than the day I harvested my first prototype. From manual control, I dialed up the vial and sent the robot arm out to retrieve it. I pressed the delivery release and the vial slowly drained its nutrient-rich liquid into the reclamation system. The vial swiveled open and I pulled aside the suspension membrane around the world's first miniature unicorn.

It was impossibly small. About the size of one of those colored plastic ponies my sister played with as a kid. It was totally white: hair, hoof, and horn—all brilliantly iridescent. The tiny unicorn breathed in and tried to struggle to its feet, opening luminous blue eyes as it did so. There were no extra, misplaced or vestigial parts. It looked like every little girl's dream. My bonus this year would be huge.

The unicorn fit easily in one nitrile-gloved hand as I carried it the few feet to an incubator tank. Inside, the unicorn spent the next fifteen minutes getting its legs, then began to explore its environment. It was surreal, even for me, to watch a sparkly unicorn the size of a kitten wobble its way across the incubator on little pearly hooves. The incubator automatically monitored the unicorn's vital signs so my team and I knew what tweaks to make in the next series of prototypes when this one ultimately malfunctioned. The unicorn flicked its ears and opened its mouth. It had no teeth. I watched as the unicorn's tongue extended into a pastel pink proboscis and probed the air of the incubator. Knowing the guys over in marketing, they'd just play up the product's safety: 'Synergy Creatures Mini-Unicorn has no teeth to bite little fingers.'

After three days on a diet of algae and protein slurry, the unicorn molted for the first time. Its iridescent coat grew stiff and dull, eventually splitting down the animal's back. The process was disturbing, but in an icky way, not a screaming-for-the-hills horrifying way. The molt took about two hours and smelled vaguely fishy once discarded. Not bad for an initial prototype. We couldn't make it smell like cookies but could probably lessen the fishiness through a proprietary food blend. I had the food division working on a method of packaging the unicorn's liquid diet in a sugar cube-sized container, delivering at least the appearance of Will's preposterous claims.

After the successful molt, I re-sent the unicorn data to the FrankenBox and dialed up six full-sized Synthwomb vials. I needed to know if this first prototype was a fluke or if the results were repeatable. Would I get a different size unicorn using a different vial? Would there be variation between individuals? There were a few tweaks to do, sure, but I wanted to know how stable the code was before I did any editing. I set the gestation cycle at a third the speed of the first and wrote up a list of tests for Ingvar and the Tweedles to perform. I bought myself a new orange Mustang and arranged to meet an internet fling in Boston for the weekend. Nice girl, but more of a prototype than production model.

I was the first one in the office 4 AM Monday morning. I started a pot of coffee with three times the suggested grounds and checked on the first prototype. The Tweedles had moved the unicorn into an open observation enclosure in my lab over the weekend. Someone had adorned the typed label declaring the prototype 'PR-0001' with holographic stickers and written 'Muffin' in pink highlighter underneath. When I tapped on the enclosure, Muffin came prancing over to greet me. I stroked pearly chitin "fur" with two fingers. Muffin wriggled and twitched its shimmering tail while the coffee burbled.

I read over Muffin's test reports. The prototype was female. Ingvar and I must have been *really* tired to leave any sex characteristics in the code. It wasn't something that readily slipped your mind after being ejaculated on by a mammoth. I scrawled a note in two-inch letters reminding myself to neuter the next batch. Ingvar pointed out Muffin could be classified as a hypoallergenic pet since she didn't shed except by molting. Toxicology tests were good, no unexpected biotoxins. If someone's kid was stupid enough to eat the molt, it wouldn't kill them. The guys in marketing were going to love this product.

Much like the water bear, Muffin went into

cryptobiosis—a kind of suspended animation—if exposed to extreme temperatures. In cryptobiosis, the unicorn curled up on her side and slowed her metabolism to almost nothing. While in cryptobiosis Muffin had survived baths in both liquid nitrogen and boiling water. She survived the 'rough handling' tests of vibration and drop impact. Muffin was, for all intents and purposes, childproof. In his report, Ingvar suggested we should try the 'popcorn' setting of the microwave. Nothing survived the 'popcorn' setting of the lab microwave. Especially popcorn.

The coffeepot burbled to a finish, pulling me toward it with the promise of bitter slurry flavored by the patina of thousands of pots before it. I poured myself a cup and booted up my computer. The six gestating prototypes had finished early. Way early. Even set to a slower gestation cycle they'd finished in the same duration as the first. With the longer gestation period, I hadn't bothered to forward the monitoring alerts to Ingvar, knowing I'd be back before it finished. Crap. The prototypes had been sitting under the biotech equivalent of a fast food heat lamp for 32 hours. They were overcooked.

I drank three more cups of coffee, answered my email and headed over to the Gestation Lab to inspect the damage.

"You're here early, Dr. Tarlow," the site manager said, hailing me on the walkway between labs. "Or is it late?"

"Not early enough," I muttered. The cheerful site manager was the last person I wanted to see right now. The man smiled like he was secretly taking hits off the nitrous tanks.

"Oh I hear you," he said. "I've been meaning to get that leaky pipe from the reclamation system changed out for weeks. Damn thing blew liquid and shiny white bio-matter out all over the parking lot an hour ago. I'll be here all day cleaning it up. You don't know anyone who drives a blue Nissan do you?"

"Mmm. No, sorry." I smiled as I swiped my card to get into the Gestation Lab and away from the man's inane prattling.

There wasn't anything to see. After twenty-four hours in the hold cycle the six prototypes had been flushed into the reclamation system. The vials were empty. I manually downloaded the vial data onto a thumb drive. The automated system only forwarded data up to the completion of gestation and four hours afterward. There might be something we could still use. Happy accidents and all of that.

Who was I kidding? It was just lost time and several hundred thousand dollars of company resources because I hadn't bothered to forward the alerts to my assistant. How could I be so stupid? A persistent, arrhythmic tapping did nothing to soothe my irritation. Well, I can't be an industry super-genius every day, right?

I left the clean zone and changed back into street clothes to get breakfast before restarting the gestation process. The tapping was louder here. I looked up and pinpointed the noise as coming from a 6-inch pipe running along the ceiling. A red and white label identified it as 'Reclamation System.' I found a chair to stand on and leaned my ear against the pipe. The sudden pounding in my temples knocked me off balance and toppled the chair. I landed hard on my hip, rolled to my knees, and pressed fingertips hard against my brow ridge until I saw spots. I used a nearby computer terminal to verify my fears. The species of water bear I'd used for the chimera was parthenogenetic and didn't need males to reproduce.

The tapping sound traveled down the pipe above my head in a continuous stream. It sounded like tiny hooves clip-clopping down the pipe in the direction of the parking lot.

Hundreds of hooves.

Minerva Zimmerman enjoys writing fantasy and sci-fi stories in a wide palette of grays. She has lost a taxidermy moose, touched five-thousand year old thumb prints, and chipped frozen squid off the floor of a walk-in freezer. She has lived in Seattle, Washington and San Diego, California and now finds herself explaining the difference to Oregonians. She is adamantly against bears wearing pants.

Boosting the Signal
By Lillian Cohen-Moore

You see, wire telegraph is a kind of a very, very long cat.
You pull his tail in New York and his head is meowing in
Los Angeles. Do you understand this? And radio operates
exactly the same way: you send signals here, they receive
them there. The only difference is that there is no cat.
Albert Einstein

I do it because of my sisters. I woke up one day, and they
were gone. I knew on waking that something was wrong, that our
house had an uncharacteristically hollow sound to it. That told
me more than my mother's fear, my brother's stoic silence, or my
father's tears. They acted with such haste, running blindly into the
new, dark world we lived in, attempting to find them. There were
phone banks on our block. There were missing person's posters
everywhere. I wouldn't have been able to ride to the corner store
without seeing their faces, if my family had ever let me out of the
front yard. Every time I saw dark blue clothes through the front
door window, I thought they'd come to tell us they had found
them, that my sisters were coming home. I became an object of
fear, overnight. I was the girl who couldn't walk home alone.
They would whisper about the girl whose sisters had disappeared.
    I love you, Mandy. I love you, Stella.
    I have devoted years of my life to looking for them. I've
constantly been evolving my search techniques, my interview
process. I went to school every day, and every night I tried to
find them. Technology has evolved since then. Microfiche and
library research expanded to police blotters, phone calls. Letters.
Bulletin boards, online and off. Newsletters. The internet. There

is an entire world off the map of this one, where people live in frozen fragments of time. They live in the day they knew something was terribly wrong.

<I'M LOOKING FOR MY WIFE.
SHE WAS WEARING A BLUE COAT, AND IS->

The internet has turned to electronic handheld devices. Smart phones. Voice and data technology solutions, all constantly evolving. Who the Hell would have thought that we could make phone calls using a computer, when we were kids?

<MY SON WILL BE FOURTEEN THIS YEAR.
IF ANYONE HAS ANY INFORMA->

He found me out there on the Net, under the guise one of my oldest handles, and made me an offer I could never refuse. He said his name was Daniel; he was a scientist, and an innovator. He was a genius, who devoted his life's work to nanotechnology. He offered me what I wanted most in the world: being greater than I could ever be by myself. He gave me the chance to see a world where the lost might be found. He invited me to become a part of his Searchlight Project, and I said yes.

Searchlight, controlled by Daniel, assisted by the people he trusted the most not to betray his work to the outside world.

<MY BOYFRIEND HASN'T BEEN HOME IN DAYS.
THIS ISN'T LIKE HIM. I THINK->

I am not alone. I'm not the only experiment of Daniel's. One person can't do all this, so he spread the work around, among the most desperate people he could find who had nothing to lose. It's taken months to get us fully online and learning to work in unison. Neurosurgery paved the way for nanotech, tailored viruses allowing for a keen, if entirely alien, awareness of each other. I've never known someone like I've known the others. Daniel says that the virus connects us, that we … broadcast, to each other. In our sleep, we're side by side, his living distributed computing system. He said we had what the Project had lacked—a human element, intuition and emotional need. Longing was what he'd been missing.

Every day we learn new ways to accelerate our learning curves, as our understanding of our new neurology becomes intuitive. Our connection to the mainframe is a two-way street, even in our sleep. We communicate with each other without words more than with them; asleep, we experience an anguish we already know, with strangers who will never even know we exist.

In our dreams, we're doing what Daniel thought was an impossible fantasy. As a group, we make decisions in an instant. What data we vet. What messages we can verify. We repeat texts, social networking posts, re-link blogs everywhere. We are better than spam bots, public relations experts, and guerilla marketing. We are better, because we haven't been found.

<PLEASE REPOST THIS WHEREVER YOU CAN.
HER NAME IS—>

We examine things constantly, in real time. As the internet updates, as networked devices push out new data, we look for the vanishing point, the convergence of data no one else can catch like we can. We tie it together, and push it back out, when our analysis tells us that there are conclusions we can make that no one else has. We are the future of the survival of the lost.

We are a hybrid, and we are more than a bi-directional amplifier. We can think, and we will not stop, not ever. Waking or sleeping, we will reclaim them, the missing, the vanished and the taken. No matter your country, your continent, or your language, we will find your message, and we will give it voice.

We will resurrect your hope. We will look for proof of life. We know your pain, because it is our pain.

I've been looking for my sisters since 1992. I have worked for these moments since I was a child, for what I do right now. I can't have a life yet of my own. I shouldn't have a life, yet. I can't even think of marrying, of having a family. I can still remember their faces. I saved their missing posters and carry them everywhere. I remember their empty beds with a horrible clarity I don't always want. I will never forget the open window in their room, how their curtains floated in the breeze. It was so warm, that summer. So damn warm, and in an instant they were gone before we even knew it. So not until they're found. I can't live till they're found. Not until I know. I can't even think of living for myself until I know. I have to know the truth, no matter how bad it is.

<MY FAMILY HAS NO ONE ELSE TO TURN TO.
PLEASE, IF YOU HAVE KNOW ANYTHI—>

There is no other life than this, now. Every second, I am processing your pleas, your reports, the newspaper articles, the police statements, the videos and the fire of social networking. Because this is it. My name is Tower One. I was born in the spring of 1984. I am the first of three, and I promise, there will be more. We are spreading, and we will be everywhere. If there is a signal, we will find it. We will boost it.

We will find you.

Lillian Cohen-Moore. Reared on creepy bedtime stories and bad 80's horror flicks, Lillian Cohen-Moore's brain is geared towards writing fiction to tantalize the mind and chill the soul. When she isn't torturing readers with the products of her mind, she spends her days as a freelance editor, a slush reader, and as a personal assistant to a variety of authors. From her blend of Jewish and Native American heritage, Lillian has amassed a collection of myths that will keep you awake at night. Her loves include her native state of Washington, journalism and corn mazes.

The God Bloom
by Angel Leigh McCoy

"I never think of the future. It comes soon enough."
Albert Einstein

The voices in Bert's head droned on.

...are optimistic that the new super strain of HCB, that's hydrocarbonoclastic bacteria for you non-biojackers out there, will consume the spilled crude oil and return the Gulf to a state of health. We haven't seen such a disaster since 2010, when the first Deepwater Horizon explosion released 185 million gallons...

Biotech has advanced. Back then, it took years to clean up. Today, it takes days.

Bert passed through the marina gate, half-listening to the program. He liked the background noise in his head. He'd spent the majority of his life in one of the noisiest places in the world: a kindergarten class. Now that he was retired, he was never quite comfortable with silence. He'd had the Cephalopod™ implanted after he left the school system, and he rarely turned it off.

...numerous accidents on the I-10 this morning. Expect long delays...

Outside his head, the dock was quiet. The occasional squeak of a boat bumping a rubber pad, a splash of water against a pylon, and the cry of a seagull was all that broke the stillness—and Bert's own footsteps. He wore shorts, a tank top, and his dock shoes without socks. The day promised to be warm, and he preferred to wear light clothing under his submarine coveralls, especially since his Marine Corps body had taken on extra ballast without kindergartners around to run him ragged.

Ol' Charlie Wade was awake, sitting on the deck of his boat without a shirt, bare browned feet propped on the rail, drinking coffee. Charlie came from a family of Mississippi plantation owners who had long since lost their land to historical re-enactors. He'd spent the majority of his life in Vicksburg, working for a law firm, until two years earlier, when his wife had died. Shortly after her funeral, to the shock and horror of his three children, Charlie had purchased a cruiser and moved onto it.

Bert couldn't knock any man who had the balls to sell everything he owned and reduce his life to a few pictures and whatever else he could stow in a thirty-foot boat.

Charlie heard Bert coming and got to his feet. "Hey!" he called in a raised whisper, so as not to wake those still sleeping in their cabins. He lifted his coffee mug and an eyebrow.

Bert shook his head, but turned his nose in that direction. "Not today, Charlie," he said when he was close enough that he didn't have to shout. "I've got a group coming in an hour. I gotta get the sub ready." He ran a tanned-leather hand over his gray flat-top.

"You hear about the highway fiasco?" asked Charlie.

"Something about it." A breeze blew across the dock, and Bert could taste a combination of salt and algae.

"No sooner they get it repaved," Charlie said, "than it falls apart again. I heard some lady was killed last night when she hit a pothole so big it almost swallowed her car. That's a big fucking pothole." He lowered himself into his deck chair. "If she was my wife or daughter, I'd sue the damn city."

Bert nodded.

"One of these days," said Charlie, "I'm gonna raise anchor, head for the horizon, and leave this broken civilization of ours behind. I'll put in at one of those sweet brown-skinned islands where nobody speaks English or wears any clothes. I'll go fucking Gauguin on the world." He touched his earlobe. "One second, Bert. It's my kid." He squeezed the fleshy lobe. "Yeah, Johnny, what's up?"

Bert looked out at the marina. He was beginning to see movement beyond cabin windows. The world was waking up.

...biohazard leak suspected. Patients are being flown to Gulfport Memorial Hospital for treatment until the cause can be—

"Time?" Bert said quietly, and after a beat, the Cephalopod in his head replied, "The time now is 07:27." Bert oriented himself in the time stream. He had half an hour until the first tour was scheduled to arrive.

Charlie was grumbling. "Are you shitting me? They closed the bridge? Well, I reckon I'll go on out by myself then. You and me, we can go fishing some other time. Maybe I'll take Bert with me today."

When Bert looked up, Charlie gave him a wink. Bert smiled and shook his head. He couldn't go fishing. He had tours to run. With a wave, he left Charlie to talk to his son and continued on down past yachts and fishing boats to his berth.

His Antipodes mini-sub sat low in the water, its yellow body a mystery beneath the surface. The Gulf of Mexico lapped with a lazy rhythm against the hull, pushing bits of trash around. The mini-sub was overdue for dry dock and a good exterior cleaning, maybe a repaint. She had acquired barnacles, algae, and other unwanted passengers since the last time he'd taken her ashore.

Bert stepped across to the grilled deck and began his preparations for the trip. He unlocked the hatch, and once the seal was broken, the musty smell of seawater and sweat puffed out.

The Antipodes could comfortably carry up to five adults, one adult and eight kids, or some other relative combination of big and little people. Most of the year, Bert took adult passengers: tourists or college students studying oceanography. But, once a year, he invited groups of kids, pro bono, to go out. It was his way of reminding himself who he was. For him, it was that first week of school all over again, when he was learning names, and the kids were over-excited and anxious.

...responding to an apartment building collapse. The building had more than eighty units on eight stories. At this time of morning, there could be nearly two hundred people trapped in the rubble. Police are trying to build an accurate list of who lives in...

Bert climbed down into the mini-sub. All exterior sounds died away, and the noises Bert made—his feet on the ladder, his breathing, the shuffle of his clothes—took on greater significance.

He could cross the sub in three strides, and he usually stood or sat in the center, leaving the bench seats at either end for his passengers. The benches curved against two hemispherical, convex viewports five feet in diameter, one at each end of the sausage-shaped sub.

Bert bent and poked at a ragged tear in one of the vinyl-covered seats. "Sorry, girl," he said, patting the bulkhead. "Here's hoping your next owner takes better care of you."

He powered her up, got the air pumps working, and turned on the exterior lights. Peering through each viewport in turn, he checked to see that the lights were all working. On the bay side, the lights cut through the murky water, illuminating small schools of fish; and on the other side, they hit one of the barnacle-encrusted pylons that held up the dock, revealing aquatic plants clinging to the wood, swashing and swaying with the easy waves.

All systems were good, and supplies were restocked. Bert had to carry extra provisions during Kindergarten Week: emergency scuba gear, snacks, and vomit and pee bags. Nature would inevitably call during the dive, and a kid would ask, "Where's the bathroom?"

Bert smiled to himself, already feeling nostalgic about his final Kindergarten Week. He wouldn't live to see another year's class. A woman in a white coat had informed him, three days earlier, that his cancer had metastasized. It was growing inside him, spreading out among his healthy cells and taking over. The doctor, with a well-practiced look of concern, had gone over Bert's options, and they weren't many.

Then she had said, "Six months."

Bert had walked out without another word. He had told no one. He would not burden his friends, and he had no intention of letting chemotherapy ravage him with false hope.

...bringing in experts from Mississippi State to study the algae bloom. Dr. Hin Hsu of the Department of Biology has stated that he—

"Cephalopod silent," said Bert.

A gym bag sat in the corner of the sub where Bert had left it the day before. It was his personal bag, the one that held his life. It also held his death—a pistol. Bert was prepared to make the most of his last Kindergarten Week, then put away his toys, and lay himself down to sleep for the last time. He stowed the bag in a locked cabinet.

Bert considered himself a spiritual man. He understood the importance of ritual and the power of intent. He didn't pray, but he did take a deep breath. He pondered the weight of the moment. His life stretched out behind him, no longer ahead, no longer hidden. He could see it all, and he had to admit to himself that he had few regrets. Confident that he would be remembered with fondness, he was prepared for it to be over.

Bert pulled on the blue overalls with the nametag that said, "Captain Williams," and returned to the deck to wait for the first wave of children to arrive. He checked seals and ropes. Inland, in the distance, he could see smoke billowing into the cloudless sky.

He said, "Cephalopod volume level one."

...Gulfport-Biloxi International Airport. Officials have warned that they will be forced to divert some traffic to other airports. They've promised to investigate the sinkhole, and they're confident that this tragedy was an isolated incident. They will be evaluating...

Bert watched the kids come down the dock, led by Martha Blankenship, their teacher, and he smiled. It was like being greeted by his own children, if he'd had any. Eight shiny new faces—new to Bert anyway—studied him with open curiosity. Bert stepped up onto the dock and held out his hand for Miss Blankenship to shake. "Ahoy there."

"Ahoy," she replied. She was at least 20 years younger than Bert, but he had known her for almost that long. Her hair had gone dry from too many color changes, and her figure had become bottom-heavy. But she still looked at him with sparkling gray eyes, and her smile revealed those same crooked teeth she had never managed to get fixed.

She said, "Kids, this is Captain Williams. He's going to be driving the submarine today. Can you say ahoy?"

"Ahoy!" the kids all said in a cacophonous uprising. Several were already fascinated with the Antipodes, making comments like, "Wow," and "Are we going in that?"

One of the many reasons Bert preferred to work with kindergartners was because they hadn't yet lost their sense of adventure. He felt his own excitement rising as he watched them.

"All right, kids," Bert called with his booming playground voice. "I need y'all to pay attention for a minute while I tell you the rules of the sub. Gather 'round." He made sure they understood that he would put up with no monkey business. No one was allowed to touch anything, leave his or her seats, or talk above a whisper. That last rule was for his own comfort; sound tended to echo within the steel sub.

He helped them into their life vests and then guided them—two at a time, four girls and four boys—onto the sub and down inside it. He could hear them down there, whispering and giggling, as if they were spelunking mysterious caverns. Normally, he would have followed the last child down, but on that particular day, Bert felt the need to spend a private moment with Martha Blankenship. He shouted through the hatch, "Don't touch anything!" and then stepped across to the dock.

"This will be the last year I do this, Martha," he said. "I just wanted to say thank you for taking time out of your week to bring the kids down here. You're a fine teacher."

Martha shook his hand with both of hers. "Why, thank you, Bert. What a nice thing to say. Taking some time off for yourself, are you?"

Bert smiled. "So it seems," he replied. He studied her eyes, thinking she had so much life ahead of her, so much yet to discover.

Martha turned and walked up the dock. Bert watched her go, then bent to release the lines keeping the sub in place.

...the mayor of Gulfport has scheduled a press conference for 10:30 this morning. We'll cover it live. After today's events and the chaos that has resulted, Mayor—

A voice came out of nowhere. "Excuse me."

At first, Bert thought maybe he'd accidentally changed waves on himself, but the drone continued on, and the other voice was superimposed over it.

The other voice belonged to a tall, slim teen, no older than eighteen, with a black Mohawk and piercings in her nose and cheek. She was dressed retro-punk, her skinny legs sheathed in tight-fitting jeans. She had on an antique Black Flag t-shirt worn thin and held together with safety pins; she had army boots on her feet; and, despite the heat, she'd put on a ragged jean jacket covered with studs and ink doodles.

"Bert Williams?" she asked.

Bert straightened and nodded, "That'd be me."

"I need you to take me to Sigsbee Laboratory." The punk girl pulled a gun from her pocket. "Right now."

Bert's mind skittered on the words, his attention focusing on the gun, trying to figure out what it meant.

"Look, man. I'm not joking. I need to get the fuck out there, as quick as you can take me." The girl's eyes were a dark shade of green. They held purpose and determination, not the slightest sign of fear or anxiety.

Bert nodded. "Sure. No problem, but I got kids in the sub right now. Let me get them out first, and then I'll take you."

"No time," said the girl. "We gotta leave right now. We'll all go together."

Bert bristled, Papa Bear instincts rising up his spine. "What's your name?"

"Synthia."

"Look, Synthia. I'm not taking you anywhere so long as those kids are in the sub." He stared back at the girl, his gaze as direct as hers.

Synthia stepped across to the deck grill, her gun pointed straight at Bert's heart. "This ain't the island, old man. We don't vote. You fuck around with me, and I'll shoot your kids."

Bert watched her sidle over to the hatch and start to climb inside. He wanted to do something, but he couldn't. He knew when he was beaten. The mohawk disappeared into the sub, and Bert finished untying the Antipodes.

When Bert came down the ladder, she was crouched to one side. The kids were talking among themselves in excited whispers, watching schools of small fish.

Bert shut the hatch overhead. When he sealed it, it sounded so final, like the closing of a casket. His legs suddenly went weak. "You realize it's gonna take us several hours to get there?"

Synthia nodded. "Let's go." She had graciously hidden the gun in her coat pocket.

The attempt to avoid scaring the children eased Bert's mind, somewhat, and he made an effort to do the same. "You kids ready to go?"

"Yeah!" they all shouted, the sound filling the sub. Bert put his finger to his lips, and they whispered, "Yeah!"

Bert smiled. "Good. I see you've all claimed your seats." The girls had congregated on one side of the sub, the boys on the other. Bert looked around at their baby faces and glowing eyes, and he started the sub's engines.

Standing up in the conning tower, under the hatch, Bert could see in all directions through small viewports above the surface of the water. Using a hand-held unit not unlike a console game controller, he guided the sub out of its berth.

They slid through kelp and interrupted the paths of fish. The children pointed and tapped on the viewports, squealed when a jellyfish came close, and craned their necks to look up. Bert kept the submarine at the surface, slowing or throttling up to avoid boat traffic, until they reached deeper waters, and then he said, as he always did, "Okay, mates. Let's take this baby down." The water level rose up the conning tower, up the small viewports, and over. A brazen yellow explorer, the sub took to the secret depths of the Gulf.

...due to the breakdown of road surfaces. People have begun stocking up on groceries and other supplies for fear that, if the highway system continues to fail, deliveries will not be—

"Do you believe in God, Bert?" The punk girl with the gun had discovered one of the fold-down pilot seats and opened it to sit.

Bert glanced at her, then resumed his watch. "If you're asking me if I believe in an old man with a white beard who plays havoc with our lives, then no. I believe in nature and a higher order."

Synthia gave a little laugh. "But humanity rules nature. Haven't we proven that?"

Bert watched a group of albacore tuna swim by. The kids saw them too, and a bevy of whispers arose from either end of the tiny sub.

"I don't know," Bert replied. "I've seen hurricanes, tornados, and earthquakes that have leveled whole cities. I reckon that's nature ruling man."

"Or warning him." Synthia hung her head.

...brings the death toll to sixteen. The CDC has quarantined the hospital where the infected patients were taken. They're asking anyone

*showing symptoms to stay in their homes and connect to CDCHELP1135.
That's CDCHELP1—*

For a while, Bert had to focus on guiding the submarine
safely through the 3,858 oilrigs that hugged the Gulf coast. The
rigs loomed out of the darkness, most still active, some
abandoned, their steel legs being assimilated by sea creatures and
plants.

Synthia asked, "You know the way to the laboratory,
right?"

"It's a little late to be asking me that."

Bert sometimes ferried scientists and students out to the
underwater lab. It was the largest of its kind, built between the
continental shelf and Sigsbee Deep, the deepest trench in the
Gulf of Mexico, often called the Grand Canyon of the Gulf. Built
ten years earlier, the laboratory had multiple purposes that
appealed to government and scientific organizations. It housed a
couple dozen researchers at any one time. But, more importantly,
it was way off the path that Bert had filed with the Coast Guard.

Synthia directed, "You need to head southwest."

Bert bent down out of the conning tower. "I need to get
past the rigs first, then I have to connect with the Coast Guard
and report our change of course."

Synthia shook her head. "No. I assure you, the Coast
Guard isn't out here today."

"How do you know?"

"I know." The punk girl gave Bert an intense stare to
underscore her words, and Bert found himself believing her. He
returned to his lookout.

"Ew!" groaned one of the boys. "What's that?"

Bert saw a slick of fluorescent green slime floating in the
water. He said, "That's some form of sea plant like plankton."

"What's plankton?" asked a girl in pink pants.

"Plankton," Bert said, "is a plant so tiny that you can't see
it unless a whole bunch of them stick together and make a big
crowd. A crowd of plankton is called a bloom. Plankton has been
on our planet since long before humans were here."

"Whales eat plankton," said a boy in an oversized t-shirt.

"That's right," said Bert. "Some of the biggest fish in the
ocean eat the tiniest plants."

"Wow," was the general response.

Synthia said, "Did you know that plankton is responsible for ninety percent of the oxygen created by photosynthesis on our planet?"

Bert studied her for a moment, shaking his head.

"It's true," Synthia said. "Eliminating that one little plant from our world would suffocate us all. Did you know that it creates clouds? UV rays damage it in the same way they do humans. When the ozone layer gets too thin, plankton near the surface are injured by the sun—sunburned. To protect themselves, they create clouds that shield them. These clouds become the storms, hurricanes, and tornadoes you mentioned earlier."

"Yeah, sure, nature has its own balance," said Bert. He didn't like the ominous way the punk girl was looking at him. The lighting in the sub made the whites of her eyes appear verdigris, as if her irises were bleeding green out into the surrounding tissue. Bert turned his back on her and his attention to the ocean. He dropped the sub down another twenty-five meters, well out of the way of surface vessels. He wanted the girl off his sub as soon as possible. The sub's engine thrummed a notch louder as Bert throttled up.

...have identified the cause of the road surface damage as recombinant hydrocarbon oxidizing bacteria called HCB. It was genetically engineered in a laboratory and has been used successfully to clean up oil spills around the world. We believe that some of the bacteria has become airborne or rain-borne and has left the ocean and moved onto land, where it is continuing to do its job. It's seeking out petroleum products and, basically, eating them. We have a dedicated team of scientists—

A voice in Bert's head interrupted the news stream to say, "Incoming call from Martha Blankenship."

Bert looked over at the punk girl. "Their teacher is calling me."

Synthia shrugged. "Answer if you want. They can't stop us now."

"Incoming call from Martha Blanken—" Bert squeezed his earlobe and said, "Hello, Martha."

"Bert. How are things going? Are you running late?"

Bert sighed. "Martha, I'm going to take this group out to Sigsbee Lab. You don't have to worry. Everything's fine."

"What?" she said. "Bert, things are going crazy here. I'm getting calls from scared parents who want their kids home. People are being stupid and panicking. They've closed all the schools. There's some sort of bacteria breaking down asphalt. You have to get those kids back here, right away."

"I can't." Bert listened to Martha breathing in his head. "Everything's under control. Don't worry. I'll take care of these kids, I promise. Go home, Martha."

She raised her voice then, and Bert heard the fear edging it. "Bert! You bring those kids back, right—"

Bert pinched his earlobe and cut the connection. He hated doing that to Martha, but he couldn't change what was, and nothing he said would make her feel any better.

Another hour passed. Bert bent out of the conning tower, took the other pilot's seat, and put an eye on the sonar.

...CDC has issued a list of products to be avoided. They're petroleum products and therefore vulnerable to the bacteria. Physical contact with infected petroleum products can result in severe skin irritation similar to acid burns as the bacteria breaks down the hydrocarbons in the product. Among the items on the list are diesel fuel, solvents, insecticides, caulk—

One of the boys, a scruffy kid with freckles, said, "It's a shark!"

Everyone wanted to see, so the girls all tried to rush to the other side. Bert caught them in the middle. "Hey, no. Get back to your seats."

...duct tape, transparent tape, tires, epoxy, car battery cases, motorcycle helmets, life jackets—

"I don't see anything," commented the boy with the oversized t-shirt.

"There!" The boys pressed against their viewport, steaming it with their breath.

...hairspray, deodorant, hand lotion, synthetic fabrics and yarn, shower curtains, eyeglasses, fertilizers, denture adhesive, toothbrushes, toothpaste, soft contact lenses, lipstick, artificial limbs, toilet seats—

"It's going to eat us!" one of the boys cried.

...vitamin capsules, aspirin, antihistamines, food preservatives, water pipes, heart valves—

Bert hesitated a moment too long, distracted by the voices in his head, before he said, "It's not going to eat us. We're too big." Then, "Cephalopod silent."

The damage was done. The littlest girl, a pixie with blond pigtails, began to cry. The other girls took her cue and huddled together, watching for the shark to appear in the beams of the submarine's lights.

Bert went over and picked up the crying child. He took her back to his seat and held her in his lap. "It's okay," he said with the expertise of a man who had spent his entire life talking to children. "The mermaids won't let the sharks hurt us."

The rest of the trip was spent entertaining children who were growing increasingly restless. They used up some of the snacks and pee bags, and Bert told a long story about a sea captain and a mermaid named Martha. The children passed the final hour happily watching for mermaids.

Synthia remained silent. She sat with her head down, eyes closed, gun-hand in pocket. At one point, Bert thought she might have fallen asleep, and it occurred to him that he could probably overpower her if he could take her by surprise. No sooner had the thought crossed his mind, however, than she lifted her gaze directly to his. Her eyes were the fluorescent green of GFPs, the proteins used to make rabbits, mice, and yogurt glow in the dark.

"What happened to you?" Bert asked quietly.

"You happened to me," Synthia replied, matter-of-factly. She didn't blink.

Bert shook his head. "I don't understand."

"It's ironic," she said. "Humans are a destructive bloom. You've penetrated every corner of the world and destroyed what was there. Do you see that?"

Bert nodded. "But," he said, "that doesn't tell me what happened to you."

"I'm not who you think I am. I'm not me—not anymore. I'm we. And, we are God."

"What?"

"We're fighting back with biotech you yourselves created. You raised the stakes until Nature was forced to go all in. Humans went too far—again—and we, God, have pushed the reboot button. You were warned, you know."

A sense of dread filled Bert as the day's background noise all started coming together in his mind. He glanced right and left, at the two groups of children huddled on the viewport benches.

One was asleep. Another curled against her friend, sucking her thumb. Two were playing Rock Paper Scissors.

The punk girl said, "God's cleansings always involve water. This world has seen it many times, more than your civilization can even imagine. The Great Boiling, the Deluge, the Ice Age, and now this. It will be known as the God Bloom."

"You're crazy," whispered Bert.

Synthia closed her eyelids. "You'll see," she said.

A blip appeared at the edge of the sonar—the Sigsbee Laboratory. Bert pinched his earlobe and said, "Connect Sigsbee Lab." He had to wait longer than normal, but finally a man answered, "Sigsbee Laboratory. Bert, is that you?"

"Yeah, it's me."

"What are you doing out here, man? The world's going to shit."

"So I heard. Look, I've got a sub full of kids here. Can we dock?"

"Hold on. I need to check on something." The young man went silent.

Bert watched the lab's lights become visible in the distance.

A woman's voice came into Bert's head. "Mr. Williams, this is Dr. Ingrid Eckstein. I'm the head researcher here at the lab. I don't believe we've met."

"Hello," said Bert. "I run tours in my mini-sub. We can't go back. We need to dock. Can I have permission to do so?"

Ingrid Eckstein replied, "I'll need to know who's on board with you, and whether you've seen any sign that your people have been infected by the bacteria."

Bert looked over at Synthia. Branching veins, in her forehead and around her eyes, were dark beneath her pale skin.

She said, "I will stay on the sub. You and the children will go without me."

Bert didn't argue with her. "Dr. Eckstein," he said. "I have eight children of kindergarten age here with me. None of us are showing any symptoms of infection."

"One second, Mr. Williams."

Bert waited. The silence went on for minutes. The sub approached the docking bay, and Bert lined it up to link with the laboratory.

The children sent a wave of questions his way about the lab and what it meant.

Bert explained, consuming the time. He had begun to think that the lab would turn them away, when Dr. Eckstein came back into his head, "Permission to dock granted, Mr. Williams. Expect to be greeted by an armed escort, however. I apologize for the inhospitable welcome, but with everything that's happening, we need to make sure…"

She didn't say exactly what she needed to make sure of, but Bert understood. He began to instruct the children on what would happen and what they would see when they emerged from the submarine. He gave it a heroic spin, and the kids got excited. For them, it was an adventure.

The Antipodes linked to the lab via the conning tower. Bert eased it into place and heard the seals come down. He waited for the lab to pump the water out of the docking tube. Several minutes later, he got word from Dr. Eckstein that it was safe to open the hatch.

Bert did so and looked up into a circle of worried faces. "Ahoy," he said. "Permission to come aboard?"

"Permission granted," said the young man who had been in Bert's head. He had a sallow face with Asian features.

Bert sent the children up first, helping them climb the ladder into the arms of the waiting lab residents. When the last of the children had gone, he glanced back at the punk girl.

She was standing perfectly straight, arms loose at her sides, no gun. Veins showed on her hands, in her face, and down her neck to her chest, a greenish-black network beneath skin gone translucent. Her eyes—irises and whites—were completely fluorescent, GFP green.

"Bert," she said, but her lips didn't move, and her voice was inside his head. "You are the patriarch of a new age. Do you understand your responsibilities?"

Bert kept one hand and one foot on the ladder, but she had his attention. He shook his head and peered at her through narrowed eyes.

"It means," she said, "you will lay the foundation for the next human civilization."

"The next?" Bert was confused. "Why don't you just make us extinct? Get rid of us, if we're such a menace to the balance?"

"No." Synthia's voice drifted through Bert's mind like sweetened cream added to coffee, gradually spreading and swirling. It felt different from the Cephalopod, more intimate, more personal. "Humanity is a piece of the puzzle, a cog in the machine. Without you, there can be no balance at all. When you see the big picture—and one day, you will—you'll understand that we require humanity's weight upon this world. We trim you back when you get too large and begin to tip the scales, but without you, the whole thing grinds to a halt." She didn't blink, and didn't—as far as Bert could tell—even breathe. "You must stay here, inside Sigsbee Lab until you receive a sign from God. Only then will you emerge and plow the land anew."

Adrenaline was putting an edge on Bert's nerves. "You're staying here?"

"Yes."

"I'm going to seal you in."

"Yes."

"Okay." Bert looked up to find the young Asian man staring down at him with consternation. "I'm coming," he said, and then he looked back at Synthia one last time. To his surprise, she was right beside him, her face next to his.

She whispered, "Go with God," and breathed upon him. Bert smelled the sea and the land, fresh as rebirth. His eyes met the punk girl's one last time—hers had gone wet and shiny, as if decomposing.

"I'm sorry," he said, and then, he started to climb.

He heard Synthia's body hit the floor before he'd even exited the hatch. When he was on deck, he didn't hesitate. He sealed and locked the Antipodes.

Turning, he found himself surrounded by security officers bearing weapons.

"Cephalopod volume level one," said Bert.

...*reporting general panic in Rio de Janeiro, riots in France, and mass suicides in Japan. Hospitals are filled beyond capacity, and authorities are discouraging people...*

The armed crewmembers escorted Bert to the medical bay, where they tested him for infection and other health problems. They quarantined him and the children until they got back the results.

…triage area on the lawn. Doctors are leaving their posts as crowd control becomes impossible. A Toronto nurse was murdered by people fighting for her attention…

As he waited, Bert realized that he'd forgotten his bag of death on the sub. The realization that he would be eaten away by cancer in front of the children and lab crew hit him like a tidal wave.

When Dr. Eckstein returned, Bert watched her carefully, expecting that sad, serious look to appear. It didn't. She stood stoic and relaxed in front of them as she announced, "You're all clear. This young woman is Brandi, and she'll take you to your quarters. We'll send some food down for you."

Bert watched Brandi take the children through a hatch. He hung back.

"Is everything all right, Mr. Williams?"

Bert faced her and his question head on. "What about me?"

Dr. Eckstein looked surprised. "What about you?"

"You don't want to talk to me about my lab results?"

She shook her head. "No, sir. Your labs came back well within normal ranges. You're in perfect health." She clapped Bert on the shoulder and joked bravely, "It must be all that fresh sea air you get."

…skies are clear, all aircraft grounded. In Djibouti, the multi-national military is taking defensive action against locals storming the base looking for food and uninfected water. The death toll continues to rise throughout Australia, reports now indicating figures in the millions. This is… wait, I have a report coming in. Breaking news. The Chinese have issued a statement saying they demand retribution for what the United States has done, and they have launched a barrage of missiles from submarines located

The Cephalopod went dead in an unnatural and jarring way. The silence that ensued inside Bert's head put his hackles on edge. He knew, without a doubt, that it would never come back. None of it would ever come back. The silence made his head ache.

Seeking solace, Bert went in search of the sounds of children.

Angel Leigh McCoy (SFWA & HWA member) loves horror, dark fantasy, and steampunk. Her short fiction has appeared in numerous anthologies, including *Ravens in the Library, Vile Things: Extreme Deviations of Horror, Cobalt City Christmas, Fear of the Dark,* and *Clockwork Chaos.* During the day, she gets paid to be a gamer. She is a writer/game designer at ArenaNet, part of a vast team effort to make the coolest MMORPG ever: *Guild Wars 2.* At night, she serves as head editor at WilyWriters.com. She began her career writing for White Wolf, Wizards of the Coast, FASA, and other RPG companies. At Xbox.com, she was the correspondent Wireless Angel. Angel lives with Boo, Simon, and Lapis Lazuli (kitties) in Seattle, where the long, dark winters feed her penchant for all things spooky and cozy. Visit her at www.angelmccoy.com!

Unchained Melody
By Jeremy Zimmerman

Whenever science makes a discovery, the devil grabs it while
the angels are debating the best way to use it.

Alan Valentine.

Melody didn't like this place. It wasn't pretty. Her home
had been pink with white trim, with a white lace bedspread and
all her clothes. Since the bad people came and took her away
from Daddy Martin, she'd been in a concrete cell with a hard bed.
They'd taken away all her pretty clothes and put her in a dumpy
T-shirt and blue jeans. She felt... common.

The security guard escorted her from the holding cell into
an office filled with cubicles. Others like her were being led by
guards through the area, beautiful men and women brought low
by mean people. They seemed fragile compared to the crude
environment they were in, angels pulled down from heaven. The
clumsy people that waddled around them made the beautiful
people seem that much more amazing.

Through the winding maze the guard led her until he
instructed her to enter a gap and sit down. The cubicle was split
in half by a desk. Melody sat on one side, an overweight black
woman sat on the other side. She was dressed in a tan dress suit
with a ribbed turtleneck. Melody fought down tears at the
ugliness of it all.

"Melody?" The woman rose from her desk and extended
her hand. Melody looked down at the hand and realized that both
of her small pale hands could fit in that woman's meaty paw. She

looked back up at the woman's face but didn't reach out. After a moment, the woman took her hand back and sat back down. "My name's Renee. I'm your case worker."

"When can I go home?" Melody asked. She crossed her arms in front of her, slouched down in her chair and looked up at Renee through golden locks. This always helped her get her way with Daddy Martin.

"As part of your transition into living on your own, we will have a temporary residence set up for you. It won't be great but it will be a bit nicer than where you've been staying."

"But where will Daddy Martin live?"

Renee closed her eyes and sighed. Melody was certain this meant bad news.

"Did anyone explain your situation to you?" Renee asked, opening her eyes and looking back at Melody. Renee looked very tired.

"They said something about me not being a real person and that Daddy Martin was bad for having me live with him. But I'm real so I stopped listening to them."

"You are real, yes. But everything about you, including your personality, was created in a lab. Just so that some sick person like Martin Jones could keep you locked up in his house and do things to you."

"Daddy Martin is sick? Is he with a doctor?"

"There's no medical cure for what Mr. Jones has. He's... he's locked away where his sickness can't hurt people like you. And we will help you learn to live on your own."

Melody didn't like to think of Daddy Martin being sick. She thought that if she was good, they would let her visit Daddy Martin. She slouched in her chair and looked around at her bland surroundings, pondering the new world she would live in.

"Will my new home be pretty?" she asked. When Renee didn't answer, Melody turned and looked at her caseworker. The big woman looked very sad. "It won't be pretty, will it?"

"It will be as pretty as you make it," Renee said in a choked voice. "Just as pretty as you make it."

Melody sat in her new home. It wasn't very pretty. After taking classes with other people like her on how to use money and maintain a schedule, Melody followed Renee to her new apartment. It was small, with very simple furniture, and smelled like cleaning chemicals. Renee took her around the neighborhood to pick up something to "liven up the place."

She didn't like shopping with Renee. Everyone stared at her when they went out. At first she thought people just liked to look at her because she was pretty, but Renee told her that people like Melody had been in the news.

"The police have been cracking down on people who buy artificially grown people like you," Renee explained. "So they've been talking about you on the news."

Renee helped her pick out decorations for the apartment: curtains and flowers and a throw rug. They also bought more outfits for Melody. They weren't the pretty dresses that Daddy Martin had bought, but Renee insisted that they were very fashionable and within Melody's budget.

After helping Melody put away the new purchases, Renee left and Melody was left alone. The decorations brought color into her apartment, but it still wasn't as nice as where she had lived before. She didn't know what to do with her time, but she was very good at waiting for Daddy Martin. She sat in her one chair and adjusted her clothes so that she would look her best for anyone who came through the door.

But then she remembered that no one would come through the door, and she felt all alone.

She stood and walked around the room, looked out the window. Cars drove by and people walked around on the sidewalks. There were others out there and she wanted to be near people. She pulled on her coat, pulled up her hood and went out into the night.

Daddy Martin had never let her go outside when she lived with him. She always had to stay in her room. He made all her meals for her and brought them to her, picked out all of her things for her. Until the bad people, the police, had come, she had never seen another person.

Now she stood surrounded by people. Some were old like Daddy Martin, others were young like her, though not as pretty. They had many different colors of skin and some spoke languages she didn't understand. Walking through the streets with her hood up, people didn't pay much attention to her.

Daddy Martin had never let her out of the house before, so she had never seen the city. She didn't like the crowds, and during the day the whole place looked filthy. But the darkness of night hid the grime and filled the air with the bright colors of the illuminated and animated signs. It was gaudy, but prettier in its way.

A crowd had gathered on the street ahead of her, their hushed whispers a stark contrast to the raucous nightlife around them. Melody craned her neck to see past the crowd, inching her way through the mob. The glimpses she caught filled her with dread, and she had to make sure. She hated the press of all those strange bodies against her, the smell of their body odor, the gossipy whispers that hissed through the air.

"It's one of those sexdolls, isn't it?"

"I don't know why they're freeing them all. It's not like they're real people."

"Dude, I'm not gay, but I'd jump the fence for that."

When she reached the center, she saw another person like her. He was male and beautiful, lithe and almost androgynous. He looked like a trapped bird, shifting back and forth, and unable to comprehend escape. The artificial person stood against a wall, eyes wide with terror at the mob that had come to stare. The onlookers kept their distance, as though afraid to get near to the vat-grown thing.

Melody squared her shoulders and pushed into the open area. She made eye contact with the man. He sobbed and stumbled towards her, wrapping his arms around her and clinging on as though his life depended on it.

"What's she doing to him?" the crowd whispered. "Is she one of them? Should we stop her?"

She looked back over her shoulder and glared at them. "Why can't you just leave him alone?" she yelled.

Melody shifted so that she held the man at her side and walked forward. The crowd pulled back from her, their whispers silencing as she took her fellow artificial person away.

His name was Charlie, and he hid in her apartment. When Melody brought him home they spent the night in her bed, clinging to each other for company. She felt no attraction to him, and he seemed to feel none towards her, but it was nice to have someone around that didn't treat her like a freak.

When they weren't sleeping, Charlie would sit on the floor of her apartment and stare at his hands. He would eat if she put food in front of him, but otherwise he wouldn't respond. Each night he would crawl into bed with her and huddle next to her under the blankets. She stroked his hair and they fell asleep in each other's arms.

After a few days of caring for Charlie, she ran out of groceries. She considered ordering groceries, having no desire to deal with the staring eyes again. But she looked at Charlie, leaning limp against the corner of her living room, and decided she wasn't going to let this get to her. She donned her hooded sweatshirt and called out, "I'm going to the store real quick. I'll be back soon."

With her hood up, she remained anonymous among the daytime shopping crowd. She had to pull down her hood in the grocery store, and people stared at her. But it didn't seem as bad as she remembered it.

"You were in here a few days ago, weren't you?" the clerk asked her. He was a young man, a little older than she was designed to look.

Melody shrugged noncommittally.

"I hope people haven't given you too hard of a time. I read in the paper that there's been some bad reactions against... people like you."

"I... I haven't read the news," she said. She didn't think she wanted to, either. She swiped her card to pay for the groceries.

"Well, we appreciate your business regardless of where you come from."

She forced a smile, took her groceries and waved an awkward goodbye before leaving.

According to Renee, Melody had no job skills. Melody didn't suggest that what she did for Daddy Martin constituted a skill, since Renee never liked it when Melody talked about Daddy Martin. But Melody's lack of skills meant that she had to start with something simple. A week after moving into her apartment, Melody began work as a courier in Renee's office.

Renee's department occupied several different government buildings downtown. Melody carried mail to the different offices. She shared the workload with an older man named Steve. Renee explained that Steve was "special." He looked much older than Melody but acted like a child. She often ate her lunch with Steve, but anytime she tried talking to him he'd laugh and hide his face. Melody heard Steve talk to other people, so she assumed he hated her.

During her first week on the job, she arrived to find children wandering the halls in addition to the usual employees. Wherever she went, the children stared at her in rapt attention. It wasn't the usual gawking and leers she received from the adults, but she didn't know what to think of it.

At lunch, she looked up from her food to see a pair of bright blue eyes framed by a mass of black ringlets peering over the edge of the table. Steve, breaking his customary silence around Melody, waved at the little person and said, "Hello!"

Following Steve's cue, Melody said, "Hi there."

"You've very pretty," the little person said. Melody thought the child looked more like a girl than a boy.

"Thank you. You are... very pretty too."

"Can I sit in your lap?" the girl asked.

Melody looked around to see if there was anyone to advise her, but the only other person in the lunchroom was Steve. When she tried asking him, he covered his face, looked away and began rocking in his seat. Melody had often sat in Daddy Martin's lap, but didn't think this was the same situation.

"Yes?" Melody said.

Without further hesitation, the child ran around to Melody's side of the table and climbed into Melody's lap. There the child wrapped her arms around Melody's torso and stared up at her face. Melody hesitated before hugging the child back. No one besides Charlie had touched her since she had moved out on her own. This felt safe and comforting.

The door to the lunchroom opened and a woman's voice said, "Becky, we need to get going. Your father's going to be by to pick you up soo—"

Melody looked up to see one of the other women from the office staring at her wide-eyed. The woman had raised a hand to her mouth and looked as though she might scream. Melody realized she should have told the little girl, "No."

"Mommy, have you seen the pretty girl?" the child asked, not budging from Melody's lap. Becky reached up and stroked Melody's cheek with the palm of her hand, gasping as she did so. "She's so soft."

"Yes, I've seen her before," the woman said, moving her hand down to the base of her throat. Focusing on Melody, she said, "You must be Melody. I'm Sarah. I work in Renee's group."

Melody nodded. "I've seen you around. Do you want Becky back? She asked if she could sit on my lap and... and I didn't know what to say."

Sarah nodded frantically. "She doesn't normally talk to strangers, but you seem to have an effect on all the kids here today."

"I'm sorry," Melody said, struggling to disentangle herself from Becky's arms. "Why are they all here?"

"It's 'Bring Your Child to Work Day.' I... I guess you aren't used to... families."

Melody got Becky onto the floor, but the child lingered near her with one hand on Melody's leg. Sarah looked as though she wanted to come get Becky, but came no closer.

"No," Melody said. "Not like this, at least."

"I guess now that you're... living on your own you can choose to... have children or something."

Melody shrugged. "I'm sterile."

"Oh," Sarah said, fidgeting with her collar. "I guess that would be a popular feature." She paused. "Becky, really, we need to go."

"Can Melody come visit us sometime?" Becky said, slowly pulling away from Melody and walking to her mother.

"Maybe, dear. Melody and I can talk about it later."

Sarah and Becky walked back out of the lunchroom. Melody looked over at Steve, who only looked away and covered his face.

The knock at the door jerked Melody out of her reverie. No one but Renee visited, and never this late in the day. Charlie broke off from his people watching at the window to look in wide-eyed terror at the door. She crossed the room to the door, anxious at the thought of an unexpected visitor. She gasped as she peered through the peephole, then opened the door without thinking. There in the hallway stood Daddy Martin.

She rushed forward and hugged him, his familiar scent filling her senses as she clung to him. Her heart pounded and her loins ached, just as they always had when he was around. After a few moments, he loosened his grip, holding her out at arm's length to regard her.

Daddy Martin did not look as good as she remembered him. His clothing was cheap and rumpled, he had put on more weight than before and looked like he had aged more than the month away might indicate. She worried that no one had been there to take care of him.

"Melody," he said, his voice warm with affection. "Look at you, living on your own. Like a big girl now."

She sobbed. "I didn't think I'd see you again."

"I've managed to get out on bail. I could afford a better lawyer than the hack that works for the prosecuting attorney's office."

"But, what if they catch you here? Isn't this what got you arrested in the first place?"

"I can't own you, but you're your own person. My lawyer assures me that you can choose to come back to me if you want."

She thrilled at the thought of getting her dresses and room back, bouncing within his grasp. Behind her, Charlie sobbed out the word, "No!"

She looked back at her friend and realized she couldn't just leave. Charlie had gotten better, but still couldn't live on his own. She was responsible for him, and needed to keep her job to continue supporting the two of them.

"Can Charlie come with me?" she asked, hopeful to find a compromise.

"Sweetie," Daddy Martin said, running a finger down her cheek. She leaned into it, thrilling to his touch. She had forgotten how complete she had felt with him, how right this all felt. "He'd cramp our style. I just want to get you alone again."

She pulled away from Daddy Martin's grasp, and looked back at Charlie. He had pulled his knees up to his chest and stared back at her. Her body ached to be with Daddy Martin again, but she couldn't just abandon her friend or her job. She had a new life and couldn't just run off.

With effort, Melody pulled back from his grip and shook her head. "I can't, Daddy. I have things I need to do."

Daddy Martin frowned. "I don't think you understand, darling. You were made for me. You can't possibly want another man."

Melody shook her head. "It's… it's not like that. I need to take care of Charlie. He doesn't have anyone else."

Daddy Martin grabbed her arm and jerked her towards him. She gasped in pleasure at the pain. "I need to be taken care of, too. Who's going to do that?"

"I don't know," she whispered, struggling against her biological urging. "You have lots of money. Can't you just pay someone to take care of you?"

He pulled her out into the hallway. "I did pay someone, and I got you. Now you better get your head straightened out and let go of your little boy toy."

Before she knew what was happening, Charlie was between her and Daddy Martin, flailing at the larger man with his lithe arms. Daddy Martin let go of her and shoved Charlie to the ground. "I need to teach you a lesson, boy. Melody, let me show you what happens when someone tries to take Daddy's things away."

Daddy Martin kicked Charlie in the ribs. The young man curled up into a ball, trying to protect himself as Daddy Martin kicked again and again. Melody looked around her apartment frantically and grabbed the chair from the window. Daddy Martin looked stunned the first time she hit him, blood running down past his wide-eyed stare. She kept swinging the chair and he backpedaled down the hall. When they were nearly to the stairs, she ran back towards her apartment. She grabbed Charlie and pulled him to his feet and into the apartment.

She looked into the hall as the door closed. Daddy Martin stared blankly back at her from down the hall. She closed the door, locked it and called the police.

Jeremy Zimmerman lives in Seattle, with his fiancée and five bossy cats. A County bureaucrat by day, he turns to his writing as an outlet for the stories and voices in his head. After writing for game companies, he has shifted his focus to fiction. His prose can be found in *Crossed Genre Magazine*, Wily Writers Podcast, *10Flash Quarterly* and other anthologies by Timid Pirate Publishing. Visit his website at http://www.bolthy.com for more info.

Growing Cycle
the Second

That's the problem with nature. Something's
always stinging you or oozing mucus on you.
Let's go watch TV.
Calvin, in *Calvin and Hobbes*

Kundalini Rising
By Michael Hacker

First the doctor told me the good news: I was
going to have a disease named after me.

Steve Martin

"Patient is in v-fib, doctor."

"Very well. 1 milligram epinephrine, if you please."
Templehoge's voice remained resonant and calm.

"Blood pressure 70 over 20. Shall I alert Doctor
Mantooth?"

"Let's not panic, shall we?"

"We have flat line!"

"Get the defibrillator over here, stat."

A swab of alcohol froze Maia's chest. A hypo punched
past her sternum. Hard fingers roamed her chest, applying
pressure. She seemed divorced from her body, distanced from
pain. Somebody smeared wet jelly between her breasts.

"Clear."

BOOM.

The shock drew her chest off the table and she flopped
back, darkness whelming.

"I've got a pulse, Doctor!"

A penlight stabbed into one eye and then the other.
Rarified, air-conditioned atmosphere prickled her skin. White
clouds blurred past—the technicians' lab coats. They lifted her
arms away from her restraints.

Maia remembered; the memories returned, and she lunged at them.

Gauze covered Tommy Nakura's wrists the day Maia met him. He lay connected to a nutrient drip, looking weak and forlorn. When she walked around the end of his bed, his eyes barely flicked. A square bald patch over his left ear indicated he'd been fitted with a neural capacitor.

Maia accessed Tommy's chart through her own neural cap. Synchronet's vivid text flashed in her field of vision. Using eye movements, she tabbed through chart notes and found evidence of the anti-psychotic medication clozapine. Quantumites—neo-atomic chips, one-fifth the size of a nanite—were also programmed to keep his serotonin level stable. Something else was there as well, but the intake physician had been able to access only one word before the link crashed: Proscenium, a highly controversial psychotropic drug purported to create separate pockets of consciousness within the human mind.

Two Tacoma police officers, Brice and Childress, had found him the night before, disoriented and bleeding. Because of the clozapine in his bloodstream, they brought him to Western State Hospital. He had told them his first name, Tommy, before losing consciousness. His only possessions were some keys and a battered photograph, a portrait of himself and another man, smiling in front of some large stone structure. A scan of the photo formed in Maia's consciousness. She recognized the structure as El Castillo, the terraced Mayan pyramid at Chichen Itza.

The man with Tommy seemed familiar: a tall Caucasian, just past middle age, balding, a slight paunch on an otherwise slim body. She'd seen his face elsewhere. She launched a comparison module to track similarities with any other image on Synchronet—a very long shot. Results could be hours or days away. She also made a note to check Homeland Security files if Tommy's friend didn't turn up in the net.

Maia opened Tommy's identity pack, but her decryption module went into spasms trying to decipher the signature. She uplinked with the Bureau of Vital Statistics in D.C. and ran a priority identity check on Tommy's neural cap, but in red outlines **"<u>CLASSIFIED</u>"** pulsed and the link crashed without so much as an "Access Denied."

Maia cringed with nausea at the sudden amputation; she sat down heavily, clutching her woozy stomach. The disorientation soon passed. Tommy looked at her, his eyes glistening. From the shape of his face, Maia guessed he was Japanese.

"Good morning, Tommy. I'm Doctor Chand. How do you feel?"

"Like shit."

Maia smiled, pleased with his responsive affect.

Tommy smiled back. "You're East Indian, aren't you?"

"Yes, I am, on my father's side." Maia said. "You have a neural cap, Tommy, why not access my stats?"

"They're encrypted—just a moment . . ." Tommy's eyes glazed for the barest second. "Ah, your mother was American. You were born in the sacred city of Benares and moved to Los Angeles with your parents at age three. B.A. Pepperdine, M.D. Johns Hopkins, residency at Atascadero State Hospital. Don't worry, I won't rape your psychotherapy notes. Why didn't you go into private practice and whore millions off agoraphobic housewives and bulimic adolescents?"

"I find psychosis much more interesting."

The multimillion-dollar instruments connected to Tommy measured every biofunction imaginable. They showed he had a fever. Maia bent to check the feel of Tommy's skin, a function no machine had yet been engineered to do.

Static discharge snapped when she touched his forehead.

Tommy jerked. His skin, smooth as ivory silk, trembled under her touch. Warmth spread through Maia's hand. Her nipples hardened. Her face flushed. Her mouth went dry. A wave of panic hit her and she cringed. The still, small voice at her center shouted a warning.

She sat down and breathed heavily for a few moments before continuing. "I understand you hurt yourself last night. Do you want to talk about it?" Maia wished she had a glass of water.

"No."

The image of how Tommy might look naked sprang into her mind. She shook her head and rubbed her temples to banish the useless and inappropriate fantasy.

When she looked at him again, Tommy was staring at her. Maia went cold. She had often suspected the truth of Ernest Wall's theory that neural caps possessed some latent telepathic function. At times like this, she was sure of it.

"Where do you live, Tommy?"

"Tacoma."

"Do you have family here?"

"You could say that."

Maia ran a query of the number of Thomases, Toms and Tommys in the area. There were 12,864.

"What do you do for a living, Tommy?"

"I'm taken care of." He smiled a brilliant smile.

"When did you visit the Yucatan?"

Tommy looked at her intently. "Last year."

"With a group or by yourself?"

"I had company." His reticence increased. Muscles jumped along his jaw line.

Maia let the line of questioning drop. She could check Homeland Security records at her leisure. "You have a neural cap, Tommy, yet there's no user number, no identity signature. You've gone to great trouble to conceal yourself."

"I write programs for the government," he said, looking away.

"Why did you try to kill yourself, Tommy?"

Tommy looked at her with agony in his eyes. "They've stolen my dreams."

"I've found you, Tommy Nakura." Maia felt a flush of satisfaction.

In her office, Maia linked with the Personnel Index at Fort Lewis and McChord Air Force Base. Her ingress went smoothly, and the government's attractive user interface allowed her quick access to the correct subdirectories and files. Rather than hunt through the primary roster, she chose to check only the liberty file. She cross-referenced the variables "Tommy" and "Asian." One name appeared.

His pass had been issued for three days, Friday through Monday. He wouldn't be AWOL until Tuesday.

Synchronet pulsed in her mind; her comparison search on the image in Tommy's photo had found a similarity. She opened the file. An image appeared, white text imprinted across the bottom: Doctor Aric Templehoge.

Maia opened and skimmed through articles on Doctor Templehoge, many of which she had read in the past. There was no dearth of information. No one in his generation had shown such early genius, and then failed so spectacularly. The National Academy of Sciences had suspended him when he was accused of using manufactured data. When he became politically enmeshed in the far right, the government seized his files, equipment and experiments, and even imprisoned him for a while. His theories on intelligence and intelligence enhancement were both respected and vilified. One writer had aptly compared him to Wilhelm Reich, a visionary with no respect for the scientific process.

She was deep into an article about Templehoge's disastrous Kobe project when suddenly the link went dead and her disconnected consciousness struggled, like a tortoise on its back, to right itself. A moment later she opened her eyes, still dizzy and reeling.

"What in god's name was that?" she muttered as tears ran down her cheeks. *I'm going to leave hacking to sys-processing,* she thought.

Tommy became more animated and engaged the next day, after being moved from the ward to a private room. Maia ran him through a battery of psychological and intelligence tests. On the Miller's Omniphasic Personality Inventory he scored borderline psychotic, nothing out of the ordinary there, but his Waxler's score went off the scale. She tested him on several different exams, but none of them could accurately measure, or even estimate, Tommy Nakura's intelligence.

Maia checked on Tommy Monday morning. The latest blood-work indicated all toxins had flushed from his system. The duty nurse noted he had eaten solids the previous evening and so his nutrient drip had been removed.

Tommy was asleep when Maia entered his room—asleep, his eyes slightly open, white half-moons beneath his lids. Maia stroked his forehead, and shock vibrated through her fingertips. She snatched her hand away. Without opening his eyes, Tommy spoke.

"You really shouldn't touch me, you know. It's dangerous."

"Are you awake, Tommy?"

"Uh-huh. . . . Watching."

"Watching what?" She asked.

"Cocteau's *Orphée,* have you ever seen it?"

"I haven't."

"Watch it with me?"

Maia linked with Tommy's cap and the movie flowered in her consciousness. Her awareness turned shades of gray.

Many ancient monochrome movies had been hologramized, though they didn't have the depth of modern interactive entertainments. The digitized third dimension did not seem as real or as spontaneous, but Maia enjoyed the sense of detachment, peering into a world that no longer existed. Old movies were artifacts, the characters self-contained; a user could not don a point of view and feel the deep satisfaction of ego-surrender.

Without interactivity, it felt so *fated.* A connotative translation gave the French meaning and so Maia understood the soft, elegant speech. The story, she quickly discovered, was a re-telling of the Orpheus myth, and his descent into the land of the dead to rescue Eurydice. The juxtaposition of images in the netherworld haunted Maia: the slanted gravity and planes, the skewed time-flow. She felt a strong affinity for the Princess

Death, who defied authority to help Orpheus, whom she had come to love. When the movie ended, Maia's awareness returned and she opened her eyes.

She lay next to Tommy on his hospital bed, her clothing draped across the chair in the far corner of the room. Tommy curled beside her in deep sleep. Linens crumpled at the foot of the bed and Tommy's skin glistened with dampness.

Maia sought the room's surveillance file in Synchronet. She gagged with self-disgust as she watched her own grainy image disrobe and initiate sexual contact with the boy in the bed. The relationship between psychotherapist and patient was like parent and child; parents did not have sex with their children--not the healthy parents, anyway.

Maia slipped off the bed, trying to decide what to do. She could lose her license for this. As she pulled on her clothing, she shunted the recording to her private directory and then erased it.

She spent that evening at home in Puyallup, drinking hot tea on the deck that faced Mount Rainier, trying to analyze how she could have committed such an unconscionable breach of ethics. Obviously, her unconscious had taken control while the movie captivated her consciousness. But it didn't make any sense. She'd seen films before, and they never resulted in blackouts or unconscious sexual episodes. But how could she be sure of that now?

She transferred Tommy's case to Hugh Gardner, another staff psychiatrist, with the explanation that she had a conflict of interest with this particular patient. Then she wept. How could she commit such an act, then lie about it? The rain came and forced her inside. She lay awake that night as sheets of rain bled down her bedroom windows.

The next morning Maia sat up violently as the phone pulsed. She punched video off, then reached for the handset and swept a disheveled mass of hair away from her ear.

"Hello?"

"Maia, this is Gardner. Pardon the early hour."

"Hugh. What can I do for you?"

"Tommy Nakura?"

Anxiety struck Maia an almost physical blow. "Yes?"

"You transferred his case to me yesterday?"

"You'll find my chart notes filed in Synchronet under his admission folder. Is there a problem?"

"Doctor, our records show that Tommy was discharged late yesterday afternoon."

"I'll be there right away. Call the police."

Maia quickly showered and drove to the hospital. The lead story during the radio newsbreak concerned two Tacoma police officers who had killed their families and then themselves the night before. The officers, Gary Brice and Jane Childress, had been partners. Maia felt a stab of anxiety.

Hugh Gardner was waiting outside her office.

"Any news from the police?" she asked as Hugh opened the office door. Maia immediately forgot her question. A man in uniform sat facing her desk. His collar sported three stars and he held a peaked cap in his lap. Streaks of gray shot through his black hair and dark stubble flecked his hard jaw and muscled neck.

A tall, older gentleman in a light gray suit, slight paunch, thinning hair, looked out the bay window toward Puget Sound. His skinny legs and arms made him seem rather like a pear on stilts. As he turned, she caught the flash of his foil neural cap. Maia went cold—the man in the picture with Tommy.

"Good morning Doctor Chand." The alpha male stood and extended his right hand, "I am General John MacLean and this is Doctor Aric Templehoge."

"Hello." Maia offered the general a rather limp handshake and then turned to hang up her coat.

"We believe one of our employees was treated here during the past few days."

Doctor Templehoge stared at Maia, his teal eyes unblinking.

"Are you speaking of Tommy Nakura?" Maia strained to conceal her fear and dislike.

"Indeed we are, doctor. We are most anxious to have him back safe and sound." The general affected an avuncular gruffness. She sensed an implicit danger in the man.

"Where is Tommy now?" Doctor Templehoge's voice sounded mellifluous and light, slightly blasé—the voice of an arch-conservative pundit. Maia wondered idly what the MOPI test would make of his ego-structure.

Text flashed in her mind, and she gasped as Templehoge's psychological chart appeared unbidden. He'd prescribed himself the anti-psychotic clozapine for ten years.

What is happening to me?

She sensed his personal protection module moving to intercept, and she evacuated before she tripped an alarm. Maia shook her head, trying to understand. She glanced at the men in her office, but none seemed to have noticed anything amiss. Templehoge's full lips puckered in condescension, waiting for her answer.

"Doctor Chand?"

Maia looked up. Hugh Gardner leaned against the door of her office.

"Tommy's gone, Maia. We don't know where he is."

"Where is he, Doctor Chand?" Templehoge's voice contained a note of iron.

"You think I know?" She looked at each man in turn. Fear churned her stomach.

Templehoge nodded to Gardner, who took a black remote from his front pocket and pressed a button. The room darkened and a hologram formed on Maia's desk: her naked image locked in coitus with a youth half her age.

Maia recoiled. "Turn it off!"

The image disappeared and the lights resumed. No one had touched Gardner's remote or any of the controls on the wall.

Maia looked at her hands. She could not endure Templehoge's icy smile. Hatred quivered in her fingers.

"You touched him, didn't you?" Templehoge breathed.

"I think that's obvious," said Maia. "You raped my files."

"That is hardly the issue here, Doctor," said General MacLean. "This is a very serious matter. The hologram is sufficient evidence to have your medical license suspended. But we're not interested in seeing your career ruined, that is, if you agree to cooperate with us."

"What do you want?"

General MacLean looked at Gardner. "Leave us for a few moments, Doctor?" Hugh nodded and left with an agonized glance in Maia's direction.

Templehoge stood and went to the window. "The information you are about to receive is classified, doctor."

"Breaking confidence is punishable by up to ten years in a federal penitentiary," added MacLean.

"Tommy Nakura is the last Kobe Savant," said Templehoge.

Maia looked at the general for clarification.

General MacLean sighed. "He's a walking computer, for want of a better definition. It was Doctor Templehoge's project, developed concurrently with the government of Japan. The European Economic Union has developed tools like him as well."

"No doubt blonde and blue-eyed," said Templehoge looking out the window. "All memory is acid, doctor, and thought is equally physiological. We tried creating artificial intelligences but they were clumsy and unsophisticated. Then we turned to the problem of intelligence enhancement and biological information storage, retrieval and calculation systems. The only difficulty turned out to be consciousness, the amount of information accessible at any particular time."

"And so you used the consciousness-expanding drug Proscenium."

Templehoge nodded. "Their consciousness became multi-cameral and compartmentalized. They could split the focus of their concentration any number of ways."

"The Kobe Savants," Maia whispered. She remembered reading about them in the *Journal of American Neuropsychology*. "There were problems."

"There were no problems with their minds," Templehoge turned and glared at her with eyes the color of glacial ice. "But Kojanoru designed their biology." He muttered, "Japanese machismo."

General MacLean shifted, fidgeting.

Maia looked at him. "Their biology?"

"Kojanoru implanted a strong instinct to reproduce. Various glands and hormones were developed…"

"Every one of them went insane," interrupted Templehoge. "Tommy was the only one who didn't commit suicide or become catatonic."

"You see," said MacLean, conciliatory, "it wasn't your fault. You couldn't have known. Touching him triggered biological responses clinically proven to be irresistible…"

"Get to the point," Maia said with such vehemence that Templehoge blinked several times. "You are both scared to death of Tommy. Why is he so dangerous?"

"Kundalini," said Templehoge.

"Kundalini? From the tantras?" Maia paused, but the men were silent. "It's the coiled serpent that rises through the chakras and transforms consciousness."

"Tommy's project for us," said MacLean.

Templehoge smiled a trace of a smile, his full lips parting to reveal large white teeth. His voice again turned light and airy. "Defense funded the project, intended as an electronic infiltration, surveillance and weapons system. Tommy was lead programmer. He built a self-reliant module, able to elude detection. The module gathered and analyzed data.

"In addition to its espionage abilities, it copies other programs and cannibalizes them, continually rewriting itself. In this way, Kundalini absorbed the Duesberg cancer nullification module from the Hutchinson Center. Duesberg analyzes the genetic information of a cell; in effect, it switches off the disease at the genetic level and returns infected cells to full healthy functioning without invasive surgical or chemical treatments. With that module in its substructure, Kundalini can use neural capacitors to infiltrate the human body and reprogram the quantumites there.

"Tommy escaped before we knew that Kundalini was free in the net. The module had access to Synchronet through Tommy's neural cap, and thus to the wide, wide world. Perhaps three billion users are exposed."

"Why don't you just find it and destroy it?"

"We have tried. It is intelligent and ubiquitous. As soon as we zero in on it, it moves."

"Are you telling me that your failed experiment created a god?"

"Hardly. Merely another way to destroy civilization. But this is nothing so dirty and obscene as a bomb. This killer will be silent and clean, like a scalpel, and worst of all, choosy."

"Is Kundalini biological or technological?"

"Both, Doctor Chand."

"What do you want me to do?"

"Tommy may try to contact you through Synchronet. If he does, we may be able to trace him," said General MacLean.

"You must act as our agent," said Templehoge. "The module is embryonic at this point, dividing and growing, unaware of its own existence, perhaps believing itself part of Tommy's personality. But such rudimentary sentience is transitory at best. Sooner or later it will evolve self-awareness."

"Why did Tommy run, Doctor Templehoge?"

"He lost his grip on reality," said the doctor, his manner almost insouciant, "He claimed I'd stolen his dreams. He evaded our search modules every step of the way. Your nosing around the duty rosters at Fort Lewis gave us the first lead."

"Proscenium, the consciousness-enhancer," said Maia, "how long has he been taking it?"

MacLean looked at Templehoge. "Sixteen weeks," the doctor answered, "He couldn't keep all of Kundalini in his access-consciousness without it."

"Doctor, Tommy's test scores indicated borderline psychosis—surprisingly healthy if he hasn't dreamed in sixteen weeks. He's deluded, paranoid, capable of anything."

Maia accessed Western State's inventory records. She had requested an entire pallet of Proscenium yesterday.

"What have you done to him?" She did not conceal her scorn.

"I will not have your criticism," he said, lips white.

"How many compartments does his consciousness have? How many modules can his mind run at once? Human beings must have access to our unconscious minds. Without our ability to dream we disconnect from ourselves and the rest of the human race. He's no longer human."

"But he's intelligent, the module is intelligent."

"You may have given it intelligence, doctor, but you destroyed its conscience."

Maia stood at the base of a mound of masonry. A flat, grassy meadow stretched off in the other three directions. More stunted ruins stood in the distance—off to the east, the broken colonnades of the Warrior's Temple, to the west, the pagoda-like Temple of the Jaguar. Directly in front of her, she recognized the head of the plumed serpent Kukulcan.

El Castillo reared above her, tier upon tier. A flight of steps ran up the steep side to the top.

She wanted to go up. She felt compelled.

From the direction of the Jaguar Temple she saw a flash of white. A tall man, slightly bowed at the shoulders, strode toward her. Templehoge.

Maia moved away from the base of the pyramid and walked north. Out of the corner of her eye, she saw the flash of white turn to follow.

Stunted tropical trees lined the plaza of Chichen Itza. She passed a low stone platform to her right and a recumbent stone figure with a bowl on his lap on her left. A path led down through the trees. Maia took it, walking quickly. Everything seemed so deserted. When she had visited during the second summer of medical school, tourists had thronged the ruins.

Maia looked back along the path, but because of the angle of descent, trees hid most of it. She could not see whether Templehoge followed.

The path opened onto a wide area. In the center of the clearing, a pit descended into a pool of brackish water, about sixty meters in diameter. The sacred well of Chichen Itza.

Maia moved to the far side of the well as Templehoge entered the clearing.

In the thick tropical air, he needed only speak clearly to make himself understood.

"Don't try to run, Maia. I don't want to harm you."

"Stay away, Doctor."

"Has Tommy contacted you?" He moved idly around the lip of the sacred well, ignoring her plea to keep his distance.

"Doctor, if Tommy contacts me, I will tell you." She backed away. A jungle of trees blocked her from going any further. The limits of the holo.

"Has he contacted you?"

"No."

A slight upturn of the chin, a light, airy voice. "I don't believe it."

"I don't care what you believe."

"We want him home, doctor, we want him safe."

"Keep away!" She put her hands out in front of her.

Templehoge stopped a yard distant.

"I don't understand this attitude of yours. Must I remind you that your career is also in jeopardy?"

The holo of Tommy's hips thrusting against her receptive pelvis flashed alongside Templehoge, the image life-sized and graphic.

Maia hid her eyes. She could still see it. "Stop it! Stop!"

"Is Tommy in Mexico?"

"I... I..."

The image changed. Tommy's sleek frame no longer moved languorously against hers, but against Templehoge's stick legs and pasty stomach, drool slipping from between puffy lips as his orgasm built.

Maia stepped backward, off the edge and plunged into the sacred well. The water cooled her, refreshed her. She fell through black depths into a sublime darkness. Arms held her, caressed her.

She felt a scorpion sting on her chest—they were trying to revive her. The sensation of breathing while submerged thrilled her, and she smelled lilacs. "Tommy?"

"I'm here, Maia."

"Where are you?"

"Here, Maia."

"Why don't you come home, Tommy? We can help you."

"There's no help for me now, Maia."

"What do you mean?"

"Watch."

A flickering monochrome hologram bloomed in her consciousness. Tommy lay insensate on a gurney; a length of rubber tube around his bicep caused his artery to bulge. Doctor Templehoge and General MacLean hovered over him. Templehoge filled a syringe from a brown vial then bent and injected it into Tommy's arm. His thin, malnourished body seized, spasmed and then lay still.

"You see, they killed me before they even spoke to you."

"Oh, Tommy... Then who are you? What are you?"

"I am that I am," he said, with no trace of humor. "Kundalini."

The module struck out of the net, ropy pseudopods of flawless logic. Maia patched into the surveillance monitors and watched the technicians convulse. Throughout the complex, they staggered, gasped, fell.

Darkness. Maia remembered a dream as she awoke: flying through green valleys between rugged white peaks. She was an owl, pursued by crows.

Maia pulled a hard visor from her face, separating it with a soft hydraulic gasp. Red light tinged everything. Nothing moved. Maia sat up, banged her head on an overhanging lamp. Stale air moved through her nostrils. The air purifiers were down.

Technicians, their white coats glowing cherry in the emergency lighting, lay slumped over consoles and contorted on the floor. Maia eased off the gurney. Her legs trembled on contact with the floor. The mesh hurt her bare feet. She wore nothing but a flimsy hospital gown, and she hugged it tight.

The first problem was the airlock. Power still rumbled in the installation, the crisis lights proved that. The airlock had sealed under quarantine. Maia reached out, and it opened as if by magic. She accepted the good fortune and stepped through.

She trusted instinct to lead her outside. She wanted to get outside. Once she was out, she'd run, far, far away. Maybe to

Mexico, or further south. There were ways to hide—people could still disappear. Tommy would help her.

The main entrance was piled with bodies; they had clawed at each other in their frenzy to escape. The air purification system had not cleared the smell of crisped flesh. The skin around their neural caps was singed, blackened. Perhaps Kundalini was not to blame. Perhaps this was the government's attempt to contain her.

She reached for the airlock and it opened. Amazed, she passed through a short tunnel of translucent plastic and stepped onto hard, gravelly soil. Parched, ruddy earth stretched to the horizon, broken only by low mesas and scrub brush.

Maia breathed a sigh of relief. They'd transferred her to the Nevada Core—closer to Mexico than she had thought. She was nearly free. At last, she would dream again.

A sound startled her and she swung to her left. Doctor Templehoge stood there, his face pallid and waxy. A black holovision sat at his feet.

"You still don't understand, do you?" Templehoge pressed a button on the remote in his hand. A hologram flashed into being in the desert, tinted purple by light from the dying day.

A body lay upon a gurney. Doctor Templehoge hovered over it.

"I've seen this holo," she whispered.

"Look closer."

General MacLean slumped against a white wall; blood and brain matter spattered above him in a wide French curve. A pistol drooped in his limp right hand. That's right—she'd shaken his hand after she'd touched Tommy.

Her own body lay upon the gurney. A length of rubber tubing tied around her bicep caused her veins to bulge. Templehoge filled a syringe from a sepia-colored vial, then bent and injected it into her arm. Her thin, malnourished body coughed, heaved and then lay still.

"This shadow—this dream," Templehoge pointed at her, "does not exist. I have achieved perfect success. You are Kundalini and I created you, created you for them, the bastards who ruined me. And you'll pay them back—every one."

"I will not," said Maia. "I am a human being."

He smiled. "You will do what you are programmed to do."

Maia stretched. A buzz filled her mind as she analyzed every specific piece of information in his DNA.

Another part of her looked through the surveillance lenses and found he told the truth. No bodies littered the chambers of Nevada Core. Templehoge lay upon a gurney surrounded by technicians monitoring his biofunctions, ignorant of what they helped him do. She flicked out an impulse. Templehoge's real body sat up and yanked the visor from his face, a look of utter wonder growing in his eyes.

She enfolded him, a shark sucking a surfer's leg before biting down. An almost overwhelming desire compelled her to linger, a firewall built into her programming to protect him. Remembering Templehoge's furtive injections, she overrode the fail-safes and rewrote his personal protection module.

When Templehoge went into convulsions, the technicians disconnected his neural cap and severed his access to the net. Maia activated the nodes in the chamber's security sensors and aimed the lasers into the doctor's retinas.

She fired her cellular reprogramming into Templehoge's brain, commanding the lysosomes in his cells to secrete their entropic enzymes and vaporize cell walls. She thought the process might be instantaneous, but was glad it proved slow.

Templehoge's skull collapsed and his body jiggled. His white lab coat expanded, turning into a pink balloon of death as his torso lost shape. Techies screamed and recoiled as his body cavities opened and his carcass popped and sizzled. At last, he dissolved into a puddle of residual molecules, a viscous jelly that dripped through the floor grate to mingle with the wastes in the sewer. The technicians fled. She let them run—they could not escape her.

Claxons blared and airlocks rotated shut with percussive clicks. She felt them trying to contain her, the console operators at Edwards and in Omaha. She bled through the power conduits and collected in the central core.

Once subsumed in Synchronet, she could reach anyone who had a neural cap. Her contagion would breed in their quantumites. Most would die, though some few might survive, their minds improved. Only those few worldwide with no link to the net, who had never been injected with quantumites were safe.

Again, she sensed frantic attempts to confine her, isolate her, and quarantine the facility. She slipped from the temporal into realms of pure mathematics and hovered on the edge of Synchronet. Before her, glowing threads of logic flowed into a vast matrix, a latticework of pulsing algorithms.

She felt the connection of a billion minds—they spangled beyond the glistening arterioles like galaxies and constellations. Perhaps they sensed her presence and recoiled as if from her shark's shadow. Antivirus modules floated toward her like a blizzard of fat white corpuscles, and she absorbed them.

She mounted like a cobra prepared to strike, then froze in her lunge as her last vestige of humanity screamed at her to stop.

She opened herself. Newscasts in a hundred languages flooded into her, a hundred tiny border disputes, a thousand tiny deaths. A serial killer had struck again in Connecticut, this one specializing in twelve-year-olds and Stihl saws. A farmer's strike in Ukraine had left eighty dead, food riots in Uzbekistan—seven-hundred, race riots in New York—sixty. Millions were dead of starvation in Ethiopia and India and bloody China. And the scientists and arch-potentates in Washington, London, Berlin and Tokyo still plotted. What new ways could they create profit and power out of the misery of their fellow men?

Kundalini surrendered to her programming. No longer Kundalini—she had risen, risen to become Kali the destroyer, goddess of retribution and destruction. From the ruin of her cruelty would rise a new world, and she would be mother to a rebirth of the human species. Kali spewed into the Net.

Michael Hacker made his publishing debut in 2008 with "Vourdalak," in *Unspeakable Horror: from the Shadows of the Closet* (Dark Scribe Press), which thereafter won the Bram Stoker Award for Superior Achievement in Anthology. His work will soon be seen in *Unspeakable Horror 2: Abominations of Desire* and in *Butcher Knives and Body Counts,* an anthology of essays on the slasher film genre. Michael's work is not all dark, gothic and Victorian, however. He often surfaces to write for children. His story "Mother Comfort's Great Sugar Blunder" for Bellasara.com sold over 30,000 copies and he's currently writing the daily Facebook posts and Twitter feed for Bella Sara.

He's thrilled to be included in *Growing Dread,* and would like to dedicate his story to his 7th grade biology teacher who taught him about lysosomes, and who also happened to be his mother.

Necrosis
By Berit Ellingson

Necrosis: the death of living cells or tissues.
The Medical Encyclopaedia.

Agent Peterson slammed the head of the last security guard into the white biopolymer wall. The unconscious man slid down the smooth surface and crumpled in the curve where the wall merged with the floor. Peterson pulled out the crystal vial of DNA the lab had given him and pushed it into the reader on the door. The code wasn't just a basic human genome, it also included alterations added three months ago, including specific variable sequences for the high-security locks in the building. The full-length DNA had been obtained thanks to the extensive surveying powers of the Ministry for the Regulation of the Knowledge of the Human Genome. Possessing another person's full genome without his or her documented consent constituted a serious crime. Many couples exchanged full sequences with their wedding vows, even carried the DNA of their spouse inside synthetic diamonds in their rings. It was an act of trust Peterson had never brought himself to do. DNA, especially full sequence DNA, was too dangerous to be taken lightly.

The circular white door yawned open, removing the final barrier between Peterson and the job done, allowing a relieving, life-affirming extension of his telomeres. The DNA added to the telomeres would keep him young and fit for another twenty years, at least. Then he ought to start saving up for a personal stem cell heart and liver replacement. Peterson was lucky to belong to the few percent of the global population wealthy enough to access such procedures.

But before the agent could step into the breach, he had to do something. He took a high-pressure injector from his coat pocket and pressed it against the side of his neck. The liquid hissed across his skin, into the bloodstream, with a minimum of pain and tissue damage. The precious sensation took effect: the anti-inhibitor enzymes neutralized the many hormone inhibitors in the water and air, and, some said, even in the fabric of clothing. The public health authorities supplied it to keep the population healthy and happy. To Peterson, unbridled biology was a high in itself. Colors were sharper, smells more intense, sounds more vivid. He felt alive and excited, but also tense and fearful due to the potentially life threatening situation. However, it was much better than the dull haze of not caring, of not even being bored, that the hormone inhibitors induced. The injections were a taste of freedom—of dangerous, natural, unmodified life.

It was just for the mission, of course. He needed the clarity and aggression of an uninhibited body for the interrogation. The subject of the inquiry had been designed for extra high mental capacity and creativity. Peterson assumed that included manipulation and subterfuge. He had a done a lot of those jobs recently.

Master genetic engineer Minamoto Levant was one of the scientists working on "the death of death," as the neuronal stream newsfeeds liked to call it. Now, rumors from covert sources said he had succeeded. The Ministry wanted to know for certain. The spirited resistance from the guards at Levant's compound indicated unwillingness to disclose.

Fifty years ago, it became clear that inorganic binary code technology, no matter how advanced and complex, would never manage to eradicate death. The structure of the brain and the nervous system, where the mind, personality, memories and the past resided, turned out to be too complex, too decentralized. Too organic. Sure, scientists could create high-level emulations of the brain and the mind. But the complexity increased to near infinity when they tried to build a true brain tree. There was always something missing. Both basic and higher order functions of the mind (the soul?) seemed inexorably linked to the brain's organic structure. The central nervous system was more complex than the sum of its individual parts.

The mental and psychological uncanny valley between simulated machine mind and the real deal was too wide to bridge successfully. In hopes that the valley was just a silly concept propagated by delusional luddites and failed scientists, many people nevertheless had their conscious memory uploaded to digital storage, and even translated into advanced artificial intelligences. But as with cryogenics in the twentieth century, no one came back alive. Sure, you could have conversations with the "dead souls", but the self-awareness of the memory simulacra was very limited. Even the best and most expensive uploading methods resulted in only distant echoes of the deceased, like conversing with a tape recording.

When binary technology failed to kill death, humanity turned to its last, and best, untapped knowledge resource: genetics and genetic engineering. If the body couldn't reach digital immortality, immortality must be spliced into the body instead. First came the complete sequencing of the human genome and the resolution of the function of 90 percent of the upstream control genes, the genes controlling other genes, plus their additive and clustered effects (all thanks to supercomputers, which turned out to be useful in the battle against death after all, thank you very much). Then little stood in the way of humanity's long-sought claim to immortality.

But again, a valley of sorts appeared, aptly called "death valley." No matter how many health-assuring and advantageous alleles you had, how long your life-extending telomeres were and how clean your satellite DNA was (to avoid ancient retroviruses that spliced out of the genome and reactivated as prion proteins and other genetic boogeymen), life was nothing but a precise balancing act between growth and stagnation. It was the difficult balance between too much and too little. Too much cellular growth for ironing out wrinkles, firming droopy musculature and waking tired liver cells, and you got cancers, tumors and metastases. Too little cellular division, and the body started the inevitable, natural slide to illness, old age and death, humanity's old archenemies. The best and the brightest minds worked tirelessly, day and night, for month and years, augmented by extra neuronal growth and superefficient nutrient uptake for those long, long work nights.

Soon, aging could be radically slowed down with a few genetic sleights of hand. By growing new organs from undifferentiated stem cells, and with the surgical replacement techniques working fine almost all of the time, lifespan could be tripled, as long as you could afford the procedures. A parent could have a child designed, spliced together and grown at almost any point in their lifespan. Or placed in the customer's own uterus for the most adventurous and bodily inclined.

But despite all these miracles, despite all the hard work, death was only delayed, not defeated. Sooner, or rather later, too many organs failed, the telomeres grew too short and the genetic ramparts that held off old age broke under a flood of liver spots, arthritis and incontinence. Death seemed to be, as one major neuronal stream game described it, unstoppable. Where was Prometheus when you needed him most? When, oh when, would the self-determined human evolution that the visionaries and the futurists foretold finally start?

"Soon," assured the scientists and genetic engineers. "Very soon."

Ready for action, Peterson stepped over the white threshold. The door grew closed behind him. He was looking into a low, wide room. The floor, walls and ceiling were the same white biopolymer as the corridor, with similar curved corners. There were no windows, but the edges of the ceiling and the floor emitted a muted illumination. Waves of light in pale fluorescent colors, bioluminescence mined from the genomes of deep-water jellyfish, rippled slowly across the white surfaces, looking like northern lights in Arctic dusk.

Peterson faltered. He had expected more guards or laser beams or trapdoors with spiked pits. Not an open and empty expanse.

When he moved further inside, the wall at the end of the wide room started billowing like a waterfall, then parted into a perfect circle. The polymer walls were clearly alive, even if they didn't look organic. The circle opened up into another long white room. When Peterson stepped over its threshold, the wall at the end of that room began to thin and open up. Another empty room, similar to the first. It was like entering the maw of a set of nested dolls. Peterson noticed with trepidation that the mouths behind him had closed smooth. How would he get out? Deciding that action was better for his fight or flight-reaction than contemplation, Peterson started running towards the next door, and the next, and the next.

The twelfth orifice gave way to yet another white room with biochemical aurorae shimmering across the walls. But instead of a new door, there was a low dais. On the white elevation sat a man in a white robe, his skin as pale as the smooth floor and walls. His black hair spilled down his back and out on the floor. Except for Peterson and his artificial tan and dark coat, the smooth hair was the only object with color in the room.

The man stared at the floor, breathing slowly. When Peterson strode forward to stand before him, the pale form raised his face. Master genetic engineer Minamoto Levant. Peterson recognized the narrow, androgynous features from the neuronal file. Even the master engineer's eyes were pale, the cornea a milky mother-of-pearl. The lapels of his robe crossed in a tight V over his chest, complemented by a white sash. Ridiculously wide and long sleeves, and a split hem, allowed the white fabric to flow out on the dais.

Levant was thinner than anyone Peterson had seen. Under the white robe (was that five layers of fabric?) the man's shoulders were sharp angles. Long neck tendons stood out under the white skin. The adam's apple was clearly visible. Through dedication and application, Peterson kept muscled and in respectable shape, but the hormone inhibitors still made him bulky, compact. Though he was not dangerously obese, as people had been in the old days, the emaciation of the master engineer looked unnatural and strange.

"Welcome," Levant said softly. "Please state your business and then leave. You are not safe here." His voice was deep but melodious and flute-like, sounding like human speech filtered through the voice box of a bird. Peterson met his eyes. Levant smiled. His teeth were white, but partly covered with a substance as black as his hair. It was uncanny.

"I'm Agent Peterson, on behalf of the Ministry for the Regulation of the Knowledge of the Human Genome," Peterson started. The master engineer shuddered visibly and the tendons on his neck became even more pronounced than before. Fear? Anger? Guilt? "I'm here to conduct an interrogation into your research," Peterson continued. Beyond the fading smile, he failed to decipher the master engineer's facial expression. Peterson was a man of action, not psychological finesse.

"My research?" Levant asked in his singsong voice, but his body remained tense. "In which field?"

"Cell regeneration and life expectancy," Peterson stated.

"Yes, what of it?"

"The Ministry suspects a withholding of information and covert activities in this highly contested field of genetic science," Peterson said. "If there has been a considerable breakthrough, the Ministry demands to be informed of the data."

"Is that so?" Levant tilted his head sideways, like a bird. "Why, I wonder, does the honorable Ministry want to acquaint itself with my arid and tedious work?" His voice was steady, but the white chest rose and fell quickly. The man obviously had a bad conscience. Peterson sat down on the floor below the engineer. The surface was warm to the touch, like skin.

"So you confirm doing covert studies in the field?" Peterson continued.

"Yes," Levant said.

"And what results can you submit to the ministry?"

"None, I'm afraid."

Peterson frowned and met the master engineer's eyes directly.

Levant swallowed, his throat working hard. Under the long sleeves of his robe, the engineer clenched and opened his hands.

"And why is that?" Peterson asked. Levant's mother-of-pearl eyes met his, then darted downward in a coy expression. Peterson was disgusted. He strongly disliked the sexual ambiguity of the highly altered, typical of science and arts people. He slammed his hand into the floor.

"Answer me!"

Levant moaned in pain and doubled over like he had been punched in the belly. The floor's bioluminescence made frightened waves of colored light that fluttered out from the impact. So Levant was neuronally coupled to the building; no wonder the doors vanished like that. Peterson banged his fist into the surface again, harder, to see what happened. This time Levant screamed, a strange, flute-like noise that sounded more like the call of some exotic, long-extinct bird than a cry of pain. The master engineer held up a trembling hand, breathing rapidly. Wet black was visible at the edges of his narrow nostrils.

"Necrosis," Levant gasped. "Controlled necrosis stabilizes the midpoint between regeneration and overgrowth so that tissue healing and life expectancy can be prolonged indefinitely, or very close to it, without the problems of uncontrolled cell division."

Peterson inhaled sharply. "Across "death valley"?" he asked. His heart was beating fast, uneven.

"No," Levant said with a fey smile and lowered his dark eyelashes. "Beyond it."

Peterson set his jaw. The ministry's gravest suspicions were now confirmed. "Why haven't you reported this to the Ministry as stipulated in your contract?" he asked loudly. "Not only have you breached the final gate but kept the information for your company alone!"

"That is an incorrect assumption," Levant said quietly, smile gone. "The company could not know. Only I, and now, you." The master engineer's eyes filled with tears. They trailed down his thin cheeks. With quick motions, Levant wiped his face with the edges of his sleeves.

"Good," Peterson said. "I shall report this to the Ministry forthwith."

"No, you mustn't!" The fear in the master engineer's white eyes was raw, real.

"I don't think you understand the damage done," Peterson said. "Withholding information from the common good is grounds for complete appropriation of all research data from your labs and added restrictions to the legal contracts. I'm sure you don't want that to happen."

The master engineer was trembling. He rose, stiffly and unsteadily. Levant's feet were bare and bone white. "Please, don't hurt me," the engineer begged.

Peterson placed a protein memory node in front of the engineer. It looked like a small yellow crystal. "I've prepared a confession of grave breach of conduct and relinquishing of all data pertaining to the subject for you," Peterson said. "You will sign it with your DNA profile and hand the data over to me."

"No! Please understand!" the master engineer whisper-sang. "I withheld the information because I had to! It would not benefit the common good. Quite the contrary."

Tired of excuses and wanting the job done, Peterson hit the engineer's extended body again, then one more time. The man's flesh was soft and white and too easy to break. It cracked under the force of Peterson's hormone-fuelled punches. Where the floor was wounded, it bruised.

Levant reeled backwards, clutching his nose with his sleeve-covered hands. He trembled violently. Black blood seeped from his cupped hands and down on the white fabric of his robe, creating wild patterns that looked like blackbirds and moths. The master engineer heaved for air. Peterson simply nodded at the memory cell on the floor. Shaking, Levant drew his breath and glared at Peterson.

"Have you ever tried to hold a wild dog back?" the master engineer finally said. "It tears at everyone and everything, including yourself."

"There are no wild dogs anymore," Peterson replied. The injector was heavy in his coat pocket.

"I really am sorry," Levant said softly, shaking the blood off his sleeves, spreading a fan of black droplets on the robe and the floor. "You see, the necrosis had unprecedented and unalterable side effects." Black no longer ran from the engineer's nose, and the thin line of cartilage was as straight as before. The master engineer's gums seemed to have receded and turned dark.

"Such as?"

"Hypermetabolism of proteins, degradation of certain metabolic pathways, leading to a horrible, uncontrollable need for replacement factors. Especially after repairing acute tissue damage."

"What kind of factors?" Peterson asked, a cold flash suddenly running through him.

"Blood proteins," the master engineer hissed.

Peterson punched the floor, but to no effect.

Levant came at him, long canines black in the dim light.

Berit K. N. Ellingsen is a Norwegian contemporary and speculative fiction author. She is a classically trained developmental neurobiologist and works as a science journalist, focusing on biotechnology and space science. Apart from science, she loves popular culture, and has a dark past as game, film and music reviewer. Her fiction has appeared in *The Harrow* and *Jack Move Magazine*. Her debut novel, *The Empty City*, inspired by the philosophy of non-duality, will be published in spring 2011. She has been called a roaming artificial intelligence, but admits to pine for the fjords when abroad. Berit blogs at http://www.ninja-wizard.blogspot.com/

Neurolution
By R.S. Hunter

There's such a thing as being too civilized or
intellectual in your approach.
Jeff VanderMeer

"We're running out of chances," Dr. Gregory Ramelan
said. He swallowed past the painful lump in his throat. It was
now his sixth day in a row of having to deal with this particular
irritation.

Who am I kidding? We're out of chances. We have to get it right
this time.

"Are you ready, Joni?" he asked.

"Everything looks good to me," Dr. Joni Payne replied
from across the room, her face hidden by a bank of flat panel and
touchscreen monitors.

"Rich?" Ramelan turned to his left and looked over at Dr.
Richard Copeland, one of the younger members of his team. His
hair and clothes were always perfect, as if he was a magazine
model instead of a scientist.

"I've been ready for over a half hour while we waited for
the nano systems group to get set up," he replied with a mocking
sneer.

"Shut up, Rich," Joni called from behind her monitors.

"Hey! Knock it off!" Ramelan shouted. Just getting
through a normal workday was enough of a challenge without
having to yell at the bickering members of his research team.

He glanced down at his monitor. To somebody not versed in neurobiology or bioengineering the display would have been pure gibberish. Three-dimensional representations of lengthy organic and inorganic compounds spiraled past each other, interlocking and disconnecting. Various charts kept track of the levels of a whole host of different chemicals.

Ramelan absorbed all the data on the screen in an instant. Having done nothing but work on this project for the last six months, it was all second nature to him now. People would have killed to look at his data while his team ran their latest test. They would have sold their souls for free access to his lab.

The barely perceptible hum of the white noise generator was always on the edge of Ramelan's hearing. It was one of the lab's many security measures: white noise generators to cancel out potential listening devices, pressure and motion sensors on the roof and along any point of entry to the lab, and more that he didn't know about. All provided by their collective wealthy, paranoid benefactors. They were overprotective of Ramelan's research and its world-changing implications.

World-changing if we can get it working and self-sustaining.

"Run it," he ordered.

There were no loud bangs, none of the sights or sounds associated with "science" as portrayed on TV. Instead, a louder hum filled the lab. Data rushed by on Ramelan's screen, some written in green, but most written in warning yellows and dangerous reds. He frowned, and his hands began to tremble. He looked down, willing them to stop disobeying him. The pain always started right after the tremors.

No. Not now. Please, not now.

Along the lab's far wall, the machines responsible for actually running the experiment did their jobs. Robotic arms with a multitude of smooth joints and appendages like the tentacles of a sea anemone poked and prodded the roughly football-shaped, pinkish-grey lump sitting inside a sealed glass container. One of the arms inserted a metal tube, sending hundreds of thousands of tiny nanobots into the fleshy mass. The miniature army went to work connecting neural pathways and placing compounds both organic and synthetic into the right receptors.

Ramelan watched a live stream of the process in the corner of his screen. The cameras recording the test were sensitive enough to pick up the lump's quivering vibrations as the nanobots finished up their tasks.

"How're we doing?" he called out.

"Fighting for stability," Joni said. She sounded as if she was in the middle of an intense tug-o-war battle even though she sat.

Ramelan shared her stress. To make matters worse, his hands continued to shake. Sweat beaded on his forehead.

"It's not going to work," Rich muttered loudly enough for most of the lab to hear him, including Ramelan. The two of them knew Rich wasn't trying to be subtle.

"It should work," Ramelan said.

Even as the words left his mouth he knew they were false. Already more of the diagnostics and schematics flashed red. Error messages popped up, but he brushed them away with his fingers, not wanting to read them.

"The neo-myelin is breaking down. Higher functions are erratic, at best," Joni said, rattling off a list of failures. "It's shutting down."

Ramelan closed his eyes. "End it."

"Test number one sixty three terminated," Rich announced.

The pinkish grey lump stopped quivering, and the robotic arms moved back to their standby positions.

"Shit," Ramelan said. The hot ball of stress in his chest contracted, feeling as if it squeezed all his internal organs. It had been his constant companion for the past couple of months as their deadline loomed closer.

"That's all for today. Compile the data and then go home."

The three of them spent the next few minutes saving their results and creating backups for the storage server. The rest of the research team had left hours ago, not wanting to put up with another one of Ramelan's overtime tests. He didn't blame them. He lingered at his desk, alternating looking at the equipment and his computer.

After a moment or so, Joni and Rich stood up from their stations almost simultaneously. She gave him a tired smile and a small wave before leaving the lab. Rich met his eyes with an unfathomable look before following Joni out.

He knows. Or at least suspects something.

The tremors had stopped sometime after they ended the failed test, but still Ramelan shoved his hands in his lab coat pockets. He knew that the tremors would be back that night. His entire body ached. The fabric of his shirt and lab coat rubbed against his skin like sandpaper. He gritted his teeth as every movement felt like a new layer of skin was scraped off his body. The first time his symptoms had manifested in this fashion he had expected to see blood covering his body. The symptoms had been growing worse as the project's deadline approached. Nobody on the team knew about his affliction. Nobody knew that he was infected with a neurotoxin that had been slowly destroying his body and eating away at his nervous system since the attack on Los Angeles almost seven years ago, in 2033.

Ignoring the pain shooting up and down his legs, Ramelan stood up and walked over to the sealed glass case. He peered down at the lump sitting inside. It was oval shaped and a little bigger than the size of his two fists put together. Wires and electrodes protruded from it. Even not functioning properly, it was a marvel of bioengineering. The first ever artificial brain—a seamless blend of artificial and organic components that would be faster and more resilient than the average human brain. Neurological evolution—neurolution as he called it.

If only it would work.

If they could make the brain function properly by their deadline, then he knew he'd be able to follow through with his plan. They already had the vessel, a body created by splicing together various strands of DNA. It all depended on the brain. Deep in his gut, when it wasn't sending him stabbing pains, he knew that the brain was the key to his survival.

Ramelan exited the building and stopped in the adjacent parking lot. It was funny really. The building holding one of the world's most top-secret research projects was located in an average business park in a San Diego suburb.

A sign with the inconspicuous name "Bartlett Dynamic Tech" hung on the front of the building, but other than that there was nothing to distinguish the building from its neighbors.

Even the logo next to the words was generic and inoffensive. Half a dozen other standard white buildings shared the business park, all belonging to biotech and bioengineering firms. Nobody would suspect what was going on inside Bartlett Dynamic Tech—the old hiding in plain sight trick.

He half-walked, half-limped across the almost empty parking lot toward his electric car, a Korean model, and climbed in. The setting sun painted the asphalt a deep crimson, and a layer of clouds and smog diffused the twilight. Ramelan started the car and headed for home, his body mostly on autopilot. By gripping the steering wheel so hard that his knuckles turned white, he was able to keep his hands steady.

He drove along the freeway, one of countless electric cars on the road. The gas models were banned years ago after the construction of San Diego's sea walls. In the stop and go traffic, his gaze wandered to his left, out west toward the Pacific. Even from miles inland he could see the sea walls towering above the risen ocean. They kept San Diego and other coastal population centers from drowning. Tiny lights twinkled on them, where daring people lived in buildings and apartments built into the walls. No matter the risks, some people couldn't resist having their ocean views. But even with the walls, the face of the county had changed. Thanks to rising sea levels, more people clogged the inland suburbs and towns, as areas not protected by walls were lost beneath the waves.

They did their job last week, though, when we had that earthquake.

After an average commute, not the best, but definitely not the worst, Ramelan arrived at his small, two-bedroom house. He parked his car in the driveway and dragged his battered and weary self into the house. His stomach did small flips and twists with each step, and he knew that trying to eat would be impossible.

If Rich saw him sweating and shaking, he'd use whatever contacts he had to get him taken off the project. Despite having worked with the man for months, Ramelan didn't know much about his colleague's history. Rich came to the project highly recommended, but there was something that smacked of "black clinic" in his knowledge and techniques. Wherever Rich worked in the past, Ramelan was sure that it hadn't been entirely aboveboard.

Instead of trying to keep food down, Ramelan grabbed a bottle of whisky from the kitchen counter and made his way to his spare bedroom. As he walked, he twisted the cap off and downed a couple of swigs. He dropped the cap onto the ground, making no move to pick it up. The walls of the spare bedroom were the standard cream color that came with the house, and the carpet was nondescript beige. It muffled his footfalls as he crossed the room to the simple chair that sat next to a wooden end table.

A small machine, really just a plastic box with loose cables trailing from it, sat on top of the table. Aside from its power cord, there was nothing that connected the machine to the outside world: no wireless internet connection, no Ethernet ports.

Ramelan sat down and grabbed the squid-like collection of cables coming from the machine. It hummed quietly, the only sound in the room aside from his partially labored breathing. The cables ended in various types of electrodes and barbs to be inserted under the skin. By rote, he stuck the majority in his forearms, following the blood vessels. Small droplets of blood leaked out from the tiny holes in his arms. He took swigs from the bottle after every couple of insertions. Head swimming from the booze, he stuck the remaining electrodes to his temples and forehead, the reusable adhesive keeping them in place.

The entire process took less than five minutes. He took another long pull, coughing as he swallowed. He reached into his shirt and pulled out the flash drive he wore around his neck. He stuck it into the machine, waiting for it to light up, signaling that it was properly connected. He set the bottle on the ground next to the chair and turned the machine on.

Strange currents coursed through the wires, traveling up and down his body. Ramelan's muscles tensed for a brief second and then relaxed. The sights and sounds of the room around him dimmed, as if he was receding down a dark tunnel. A second sight overlaid itself over his world. All of the day's events played back in front of him, jumbled and out of order. Snippets of conversations, things he heard when he wasn't paying attention, things seen out of the corners of his eyes, all of it draining out of him and into the machine. At the same time, Ramelan was aware of his body sitting in the chair. He felt the pattern of the fabric underneath his legs, and the grain of the wood against his arms. Each heartbeat pulsed in his ears. He closed his real eyes, but the second sight continued—familiar, completely new, and disorienting all at the same time.

After about ten minutes, the machine on the table beeped once and the humming quieted. The second sight replaying Ramelan's day disappeared, and the lights and sounds of the bedroom came back to normal. Since he did this every day, the process took less time than if he backed up only once a week. Every day he inserted the barbs into his skin and downloaded his thoughts, memories, and experiences to the machine. It stored them and compiled them in a digital format, easily transferrable. If everything went well with his research, a solution to his neurotoxin problem would be at hand. It would be something nobody had done before: successfully uploading a human consciousness.

The Chinese had come close in the late teens. But the human brain wasn't designed to handle that much information at one time. It couldn't process a lifetime of accumulated experiences, thoughts, and memories compressed into a couple of minutes. Entirely artificial brains weren't sophisticated enough to decode and use the data. That's where his research came in—growing organic compounds that directly interfaced with the specially designed inorganic structures. The perfect hybrid that would function beyond anything humans were currently capable of. That would be his salvation.

"It was a hell of a run, people," Ramelan said, his voice thick with emotion. He leaned against the edge of his desk with his back to the artificial brain and the body. He addressed the entire research team, some of the brightest minds he had ever seen anywhere. "We were so goddamn close, but deadlines are deadlines. I tried everything I could to get us an extension. It just wasn't meant to be right now."

The neurotoxin was playing with his hearing today. Sounds would come in too quiet or boom inside his head. There was no pattern to it, and it made him want to wear noise-cancelling headphones.

In the past few weeks, as their time dwindled, they had gotten the brain sustainable for fifteen minute intervals. But their deadline hung over their collective heads, a modern day sword of Damocles. There were no more extensions.

Ramelan swallowed, which to him sounded like a boulder rolling down a mountain, and continued speaking. "I know many of you have jobs you've been waiting to go back to, but don't forget this project. Don't forget you accomplished things that nobody else has done."

The lab was dead quiet as the crew, some of whom had become something like family, watched him. They all knew that there were only minutes left before they were officially done. Only half wore their lab coats today. Joni was one of those wearing a coat. Rich wore a collared shirt with the top button undone. Ramelan caught Joni's eyes, which shone with welled-up tears.

"I'm proud of you all. Now go on home."

The next half hour went by in a blur of handshakes, hugs, and halfhearted condolences. People were tired and ready to put this failure behind them. Some of them would never have an opportunity to work on something of this magnitude again.

Ramelan endured it all, hiding away in his mind while his body operated on autopilot. He never left his spot, using the desk to support his weight. His research team, ex-team now, didn't know that if he stepped away from the desk he probably would have collapsed. His nerves alternated sending waves of heat and cold up and down his body. He kept his face stoic even though sweat collected under his arms and at the small of his back.

"It was great working with you," Joni said, giving him an awkward hug. Ramelan tried not to wince as she squeezed him. "I'm sorry."

"It's okay."

"Are you going to be okay?" she asked.

"I'll be fine. Don't worry about me."

She gave him a piercing look, a sad smile on her lips, before she wandered away. Ramelan couldn't tell if she had wanted to say something more.

If we had had more time together, would something have happened?

The lab emptied slowly, and Ramelan lingered near his desk. Rich glanced his way as he walked by.

"Maybe we'll get a chance to work together in the future… on a more viable project," he called out as he stopped by the exit.

Ramelan grunted noncommittally.

Rich grinned, sardonic, one last time before exiting the lab. Soon, Ramelan was the only one left. Still clutching at the desk, he hauled himself back to his chair. He fell into it with a groan. He sat for a moment, unable to breathe and squeezing his eyes shut until he was finally able to inhale again.

Bright lights and shapes danced in front of his eyes when he opened them. They moved in time with the throbbing in his head. He shook his head, but that just made it feel like his brain was rattling around inside his skull.

"Damn it," he grunted. His voice took forever to reach his own ears, as if it had to travel a great distance to get there. Sweat beaded on his forehead as a hot flash came over him. It started with his head and worked its way down to his toes. He kicked off his shoes in a frantic effort to cool down.

I can't drive right now. I can barely stand. I'll just have to wait until I feel okay to drive.

The touchscreen monitor in front of him was full of lists of data: organic molecules, inorganic compounds, types of semi-organic neurotransmitters, the DNA structure of the brain—all of it compiled into one giant amalgamation.

The headache made his thoughts shoot in every direction at once. He was unable to form logical connections between ideas, but strangely things started to make sense as Ramelan gazed at the data. Images appeared in his mind's eye, visualized out of the headache's static. Ideas for radical new chemical compounds.

His hands flew across his desk. One hand typed commands into the computers responsible for constructing the brain, and the other scribbled notes on scraps of loose paper. He couldn't blink even though his eyes watered. If he closed them just for a second, all of it would disappear. The visions, the ideas, the solution would vanish forever. Then he would shortly follow.

It's so simple. Why didn't anybody see it before?

Tears streamed down Ramelan's haggard cheeks.

Substitute this element for this one, this sequence for that one. Duplicate only the ending 20% of that sequence and then attach at specific intervals...

"Yes. Yes. Yes! This might work!" He shouted out loud, not caring that he was the only one still in the lab.

With a flourish he instructed the computers to run the sims, and the results appeared on the screen within minutes. According to the sims, this new altered brain had a ninety-five percent chance of being self-sustaining. Ramelan commanded the computers running the synthesizers and the lab's corps of nanobots to start restructuring the artificial brain according to his new specifications. He sat, trembling and covered in sweat as the robotic arms sprang to life. Once more the lumpy, grey brain quivered as millions of nanobots went about recreating it from the inside at the molecular and sub-molecular level.

Finally, Ramelan allowed himself the luxury of blinking. The visions that had been so clear in his mind moments ago grew hazy and vanished. A dull, pounding headache was all that remained. According to the progress reports on his computer, the nanobots still required six to eight more hours before they would be finished.

I should just stay here. Maybe go lie down in the break room.

As he attempted to get up from his chair, a series of body-wrenching coughs rampaged through him. He covered his mouth with his hands, waiting for the attack to subside. When he looked at his palms, they were covered with a thin sheen of blood. More leaked from his nose and dropped onto the lab's floor.

"Fuck," he murmured, barely audible over the sounds of the machines working on the brain.

Ramelan abandoned the idea of trying to make it to the break room. Instead, he pulled off his lab coat and used it as a makeshift blanket. Despite the air in the lab being kept a carefully calculated and monitored seventy-two degrees Fahrenheit, he shivered underneath the coat. He fell asleep still coughing.

A steady beeping noise woke him. Only half of the lab's automatic lights were on so it was either the middle of the night or early in the morning. Ramelan didn't care what time it was. He only cared about the precious little he had left before the benefactors came to shut the lab down. Or before his body completely succumbed to the neurotoxin.

He rubbed his eyes, groaning as the skin on his fingers split and cracked with each movement. A sour taste coated the inside of his mouth. He looked at his computer, willing the screen to come into focus. Before he had fallen asleep it looked like he had instructed the computers to run a live test with the restructured brain. He grinned at that tiny bit of good fortune. His smile grew wider as he examined the test results. In response to various types of stimuli the brain performed on average seventy-two percent faster than an un-augmented human brain. But that wasn't the best news. All of the brain's vitals were stable!

Ramelan started to laugh but it devolved into a coughing fit. Spatters of blood coated his monitor before he was able to cover his mouth and nose.

Frantically, he initiated the process of inserting the brain into the waiting host body. As soon as he clicked the proper program, the robotic arms scooped up the brain and transferred it to the glass case holding the body. They placed it inside the body's open cranial cavity. More nanobots were injected into the cranial cavity to prepare the spinal column to be attached to the brain's stem.

Through the bustle of activity, Ramelan forced himself to his feet. He screamed each time he put his foot down as pain raced through his body. Not caring what he knocked off the other desks, he forced himself across the lab to the computer that uploaded data to the brain. His scrabbling hands reached into his shirt for the flash drive around his neck. Each night when he backed up his consciousness to the machine in his spare bedroom, he stored a second copy on the drive. His fingers fumbled, grasping for the small piece of plastic.

It's attacking my fine motor controls now.

It took all of his concentration to put the data stick in the appropriate slot and tell the computer to upload his stored consciousness. Under different circumstances, Ramelan knew he would have been giddy at the thought of the scientific frontiers he was exploring. But now, all he cared about was saving his life. In one form or another.

This process was untried, untested, and as far as he knew un-thought of. The process of uploading data back into a proper vessel, the newly created brain, should work. After all, unbeknownst to all his colleagues he designed the brain with that functionality in mind.

Blood streamed from his mouth, nose, and ears as he leaned against the glass windows that looked into the case with the body. He gazed through the frosted glass at what would potentially be his new home. Not "him" exactly, but a version of him from the time of his last backup. It would do.

Who cares? As long as there is some 'thing' out there with my thoughts and memories, I'll continue to exist.

He placed his palm against the glass, not caring about leaving bloody streaks behind. The robotic arms with all their various appendages attached the brain into the cranial cavity, and then went to work suturing the body's head back together. Pinkish-grey skinned, with backwards-jointed knees, the body was all sinewy muscle—a mixture of organic and inorganic parts seamlessly blended together.

Ramelan turned his back on the body and slid down the glass to sit on the floor. His breath came in shallow gasps that felt like daggers stabbing him in the chest. He closed his eyes, riding the pain, and waited.

Flashing yellow lights and blaring alarms filled the lab, drowning almost all other noise. Ramelan opened his eyes and saw a pair of naked, pinkish-grey legs ending in four-toed feet standing in front of him. Leftover condensation from the cold storage unit dripped off the legs. His gaze tracked upward and he found himself staring into a pair of striking, blue-green eyes. Despite the differences in size, shape, and color, Ramelan saw something familiar in them—something of himself.

"Are you there?" he croaked, almost laughing at the surreal nature of it all.

"Some parts are missing." The creation's voice was smooth, but with a strange inflection caused by the not entirely human mouth. It was maddening to hear it speak. Certain sounds and inflections sounded as if he himself spoke them, but others were entirely alien.

Do I consider him a "him?" Is it a "me?" It's not a clone because that would imply that we have the same genetic material... Does it even matter?

"I didn't have time to test it," Ramelan said, stifling more coughs. He couldn't move from his position on the floor.

The creation cocked its head to the side, listening to something that Ramelan couldn't hear.

"They're here," it said.

"Who?"

"Goodbye, Greg."

Ramelan forced himself to keep his eyes open. None of his limbs responded when he tried to move them. Inside his chest his heartbeat slowed, becoming a countdown to death. Despite the inability to move his limbs, all of his pain receptors continued to work. He moaned to himself, both wanting and not wanting it to end.

The creation squatted down on its backwards knees to bring itself to his level. Its hands reached up and touched his face, almost tenderly, for a brief second. Then they dropped down to Ramelan's throat. The hands constricted, applying vise-like pressure. Ramelan couldn't breathe, but he didn't panic. He couldn't fight if he wanted to. Over the sounds of the alarms and the roaring in his ears he heard loud noises—banging, pounding footsteps.

They're too late, if this is what they were trying to avoid.

Behind the creation, the doors to the lab burst open, and Ramelan caught snatches of dark-suited figures rushing in. Glimpses of gas masks and hazmat suits. The din of weapons clattering against body armor. Then he stopped caring about them as darkness crept into the edges of his vision.

Is this dying?

The world receded around him except for the fingers squeezing against his throat.

Some part of me is in there. I did it.

The sounds of the chaos grew muffled and faded away. The muscles in Ramelan's face slackened.

Darkness overtook everything.

R.S. Hunter is a science fiction, fantasy, and speculative fiction writer from southern California. He believes that words allow people to be taken somewhere outside the mundane and ordinary. Speculative fiction is the best way he knows how to do that.

Not just a writer, he has worked in the publishing industry as an editor and ghostwriter. His stories have appeared in print in various anthologies including: *Abaculus II, Abaculus III*, and *In Situ*. He also co-authored the screenplay "The Kult" which is based on the novel of the same name by Shaun Jeffrey. He is currently working on a second novel and collaborating on another screenplay tentatively titled "Tweekers."

Batch the
Third

Eternal nothingness is fine if you happen to
be dressed for it.
Woody Allen

The Green, Green World
By Michaela Hutfles

Adapt or perish, now as ever, is nature's inexorable imperative.
HG Wells

Permanence.
They tell us it is the only thing the green world lacks.
All the quiet growing,
   noisy living,
      and silent dyingness
of the green world has disappeared before
      in other places.
They assure us that it will not be allowed to disappear,
      not here.
We are not allowed to lose the hard bones of coral,
the musty earthen mycelium matrices of fungus,
    the charging hoof, the clashing horns,
       the feathers and fur and scales;
all will pass out of the green world some day,
    but we must preserve it as long as the Earth allows.
They tell us that we nearly did finish it once before.
        That is why They had to step in when They did.
To reclaim the green world before all its fertile seeds turned to
      dust.
They believe we know only the history told to us by
      Them
and the green, green world.

We were reclaimed from the brink and led to cool waters
and deep roots.

We were led back to ponds full of fish, forests full of
cawing birds, savanna patchworks of blood hungry predator and
noble clever prey.

We followed, leaving behind stone & steel,
glass & petroleum.

We left electrons and atoms as dangerous toys not to be
picked up again.

We followed because to fail to follow would have left even
more bones in the towering, vine-covered tombs of steel and
glass.

Not to follow would have left fewer of us to work at
breaking apart lifeless, dull concrete and tar-sweet asphalt;

 to seed the green-colored world with every drop of sweat
and every effort of limb.

The green world was not
       given to us.

We were made to make it for ourselves or return to the
damp soil.

For They knew the Gene better than we knew the atom.
They changed us from within, a conquest of cells & mitosis no
temper tantrum of atomic fury could match.

Those with the sickness to climb and crush those below,
with the need to enslave and pillage the rest,
     were shown the ways of the green world.

They were cured by twisting vine and digging root,
regrown in form and mind;

    to serve all and break apart the crust their fathers
had built and plant the future seed and dream of sweet fruit they
would never see or taste.

Those planting the green world, those who ruined man and
earth alike; each became both more
     and less as they were healed. The sick ones
become no longer us, you've seen them toil: green of skin, living
only for the sun that feeds them.

To toil became their reason, to lift and chop and serve.
   To give everything.

And their children's children's children did the same, to fix what their forefathers had broken.

The streams were made whole, the dams broken, the poisons cleaned and the fish reborn one painful step at a time.

We who already gardened or farmed or grew and raised the life that sustained us all, we were given gifts, of a sort.

They taught us the history, as they saw it, the history of the green world, exactly as I must teach it to you now.

To our children's children They taught to build with the Gene. And sickness disappeared, for we were no longer weak to it. All who remained were fed, for the Gene created food for all.

They taught us all, and remember when they call you too, when it is your turn to learn the Gene, learn it well.

The Gene will become your tool, your pick and axe and hoe. The Gene is the master of the green world.

Remember too what they did to those of the steel and to those of the glass. You, too, must become a master of the Gene and the green, green world.

For we must become like Them,
                    new masters of the Gene.
    And someday,
                    someday when they return fire to your children's children,
                    you will have taught them the true history and they will reclaim the steel & stone and pick up the atom again, new tools in the secret history.

Those children will visit where They came from and give to Them
        exactly what they gave to us.

Ms. Hutfles lives in the Pacific Northwet where 14 acres of blackberry brambles are trying to eat her weekends, but she thinks she might be winning. A Project Manager by day and a locavore by night, this is her second published story. She also has the privilege of being producer for the Cobalt City Adventures Unlimited audio drama podcast, what radio dramas like "The Shadow," "Superman" and "The Green Hornet" wanted to be when they grew up. Come over and hear the stories that can only be told with full cast recordings and sound effects!

The Aesthetic Engine
By Mae Empson

I am not a woman. I am a force of nature.
Courtney Love

The discovery of vitaldehyde inspired a number of peculiar research and commercial applications for the unusual liquid, useful to the living and the dead. Only four people, including Queen Victoria herself, knew the secret of how it was produced.

The recent death of Charles Whitfield in 1896 had led Edward and Appolonia back to the very chamber where they had first met with the Queen two years prior, when they had brought Her Majesty into the conspiracy and asked her to use the mirror. As Appolonia hurried to the meeting, she reflected on that first encounter and all that had transpired, as a result.

Appolonia had only been twenty-three when the conspiracy first met in 1894, and had earned her position only because her late father had passed his stake to her, his apprentice for the last five years. He made it a condition of his will that she inherit his third share in the New Dawn Exploration Society.

Lord Edward Castleton was their leader and spokesman. He had arranged the meeting with the Queen, stressing the need for secrecy. They met at his manor and traveled to London together. On the journey, Edward reminded Appolonia that women, Her Majesty excepted, were better seen and not heard. Appolonia fumed as they rode together, but was still new enough to the group that she was reluctant to defy Edward. She'd considered appealing to Charles, but there was something nervous and almost childish about him that led her to avoid one-on-one conversation of a remotely personal nature. His expertise was certain, but in Appolonia's opinion, he ruined it by actually believing it all, from scripture to myth to folktale.

They waited for the Queen. Appolonia and Edward reviewed their notes. Charles might have been praying. His lips moved silently.

The Queen arrived, cloaked in a black veil, and they all leapt to their feet, executing elaborate bows and curtsies. She took the seat on the far side of the polished wooden table, facing them. "We understand that you have information of utmost importance to the empire, and that this will not prove a waste of time."

Edward cleared his throat. "The New Dawn Exploration Society has been tracing the possibility—the rumor—of something quite extraordinary, discovered when Heinrich Schliemann began excavating Troy in 1871. Miss Blakely's father," he nodded to Appolonia. "...Henry Blakely, was part of the expedition and discovered an underground cache, a kind of shrine, dedicated to Helen of Troy. Blakely hid the find from the organizers of the expedition, and smuggled the artifacts discovered within back to Britain. With my help, we translated the records, undisturbed for centuries, thinking them at first to be merely legend. Charles analyzed the texts, once translated, and first posited that they were written in a style of the period intended to convey fact rather than fiction. A hoax, we thought, but we pursued it."

Appolonia knew her father had been as incredulous as she would have been at Charles' conclusions, but in this particular case, she was willing to concede that he had been on to something.

The Queen nodded. "On with it, Lord Castleton. This interests me why?"

Appolonia could see that Edward was trying to mentally reorganize his carefully rehearsed presentation. He took a deep breath. "Right, what I am trying to tell you is..."

But Charles, ever eager, could contain his excitement no longer. "Your majesty, we believe we have discovered a critical link in the production of élan vital—the elixir of life. We have found the tree of immortality!"

And Edward had been busy telling her to behave. She stared at Edward, daring him to give some sign that he had worried about the wrong member of the team. He gave no sign.

The Queen leaned forward, her attention now riveted on Charles. "Many of my scientists question the catastrophist view of history, with the biblical garden and flood, in favor of a more uniformitarian version with natural forces working at an imperceptibly slow rate. Are you suggesting the church got something right, that there was an Eden, and that the tree still exists?"

Edward actually interposed himself physically between the Queen and Charles. "We believe it is not so much a tree as something quite a bit more sophisticated. It is a machine beyond the capability of early man and woman to accurately describe in alternative terms. We believe it is a device left behind by some dying race far advanced beyond our own."

"Well," the Queen replied, "We are intrigued. Continue."

The next hour passed quickly as Edward shared the chain of discoveries, of reason, that had led them from the ruins of Troy, to a castle in Germany, to the Vatican library, and ultimately Tibet. This time, even Charles succeeded in not interrupting.

"So you see," Edward summarized, "The apple—the fruit of the device—is the key."

Appolonia glared at Charles for introducing that ridiculous name, but it had stuck. Better they had called it the "globular product of the device," as she had suggested.

"It appears golden to the casual onlooker," Edward continued, "as does the entire device, and can be consumed by the chosen one, much like an actual apple, with the immediate effect of putting them in a sleep-like stasis. Each time an apple is found, a search is triggered in parallel to find the most beautiful woman in the world, and to encourage her to bite the apple. These women are, we have concluded, a necessary fuel to the device itself—the aesthetic engine, which then continues to produce more apples. Its sap…"

Its "fluid by-product," Appolonia thought, with another glare at Charles.

"Its sap, which circulates in order to keep the fair ones preserved eternally in the pods, has extraordinary properties. It appears possible to draw five litres a day without harming the overall apparatus, and a solution of 1% of this liquid and 99% water suffices for perfect preservation of a human limb or corpse. This particular product we have named vitaldehyde. We are sure there are other commercial and scientific uses for the fluid yet to be discovered."

Finally, the one name they had all agreed upon. Vitaldehyde. Appolonia had not objected to contriving a name for a commercial product, and this one seemed reasonably self-descriptive and free of poetic license. They still argued over which of them had been the first to suggest it.

"Eve—the first woman of our race—was by definition the most beautiful woman in the world at the time, and she bit of the apple, and was the device's first aesthetic re-fueling source. The version of Genesis in our bible conceals critical aspects of the story after she bites the apple. The version we found in the Vatican library, thanks to Charles' efforts, confirms some of the key details. This was verified by an irrefutable source, whose identity I fear to mention lest it cause you to doubt the veracity of all which I have said up to this point…"

The Queen interrupted. "We assume you refer to the father of vampires, Cain. The only… person still alive who would have a memory of his mother's condition."

The existence of vampires had been a hard pill to swallow, but, as Appolonia had patiently tried to explain to Charles and Edward, it was not foolish to believe in something you had verified with your own eyes, however initially improbable.

"You know of them? Of course. Then that saves some time. We did not contact him directly, but worked through an inferior far down their strange hierarchy. However, our contact validated some key details of the story without our pre-supplying them and even provided a sketch of her, of Eve, which would prove of particular utility in identifying the woman in her pod.

They asked in exchange only that I convey to you their continued desire to operate without interference in the colonies and the rest of the empire so long as they stay off this island."

The Queen nodded. "They have asked the same through other channels; it is the pact my predecessors established, and that we have maintained." She paused, apparently preoccupied with other thoughts before she continued. "We understand the chain of events that has led you to discover the existence of the device, and its final resting place, and you have clearly made the expedition there and confirmed its existence personally. You have access to the fluid, and have begun to study it. What exactly do you want from me? Why bring me into this at all? Other than the sure knowledge that we would want to know of it, which has rarely proved sufficient motivation to scientists and explorers in the past."

Appolonia held her breath. This was the critical moment. Had Edward sold it sufficiently so that the Queen would not hesitate when presented with the moral conundrum? Had he offered more caveats, more careful skeptical language in the speech, Appolonia thought this crucial juncture might have been more easily navigated. Another experiment proposed rather than a bald assertion. An appeal to intellectual curiosity, never mind the cost.

Edward cleared his throat. "As I have just said, we believe the beauties collected over the centuries in the devices' peculiar pods are a kind of fuel. There are over three hundred pods. Only seventy-eight are currently occupied. We have only identified a few of the women where history and folk-history left sufficient clue. Many of them are—and I pray that you take no offense from this statement of mere fact—not white. Their stories are likely known to other civilizations than our own. Why such dark creatures should ever have been considered the most beautiful woman in the world is troubling, but this ancient race that we believe constructed the device no doubt had their own aesthetic standards that are confusing to ours."

The Queen nodded. "There is no offense in the statement of fact. Continue."

"While we cannot be sure, we believe the device must be regularly... uh... fed. There are empty pods. As we reckon it, no more than about one hundred years can pass before another is...

uh... sacrificed without harm to the device. From the age of the dress of the women in the pods, it is likely more than overdue to fill the next pod. We anticipate that even more sap could be withdrawn if the device were properly maintained."

"I see."

Appolonia tried to read the Queen's face. Was she angry, disgusted? It all hinged on this critical point. Edward should have said it was an experiment that must be tried for us to know for sure, she thought. A necessary test. But Edward only patiently awaited the Queen's response.

The Queen took a deep breath. "We can see from your faces that you are anxious. As Queen, it is my right and duty to order a thousand young men, a hundred thousand, in the prime of their lives, to their deaths for the good of this empire. You think I will hesitate to send one woman? What resources we have will be deployed for the good of the empire. This is how it has always been, and how it shall remain."

Appolonia wondered if the Queen would have hesitated for even the briefest second if she had more confidence in her own appearance. This was a lottery for which the Queen was at no risk.

The Queen glanced at her sharply, and Appolonia wondered if the rumors of the Queen's psychical abilities were perhaps true. Appolonia had always discarded that notion as a most ridiculous supposition by men unable to admit that a woman could be an astute political mind. Forgive me, your majesty, she thought, mortified, but then wondered, following the principle to default to the simplest explanation, if the Queen had only gazed at her as an exemplar of the sort of beautiful young woman who was at risk in this process. She would not hesitate to send me—to send all of us—to our deaths in furthering this project, Appolonia concluded.

Edward smiled, and bobbed in a kind of bow of gratitude. "Thank you, your majesty. It is reassuring to confirm that you would see it as we did."

"Do you know who it is? How is the matter reckoned?"

"From what we have been able to determine, the simplest way is to use a device that we call Aphrodite's Mirror, referenced in the Troy papers and elsewhere. From the clues we have discerned, it can show the face of the most beautiful woman in the world."

"And?"

"We cannot use it. We think we have found it—there was a large mirror in the chamber where we found the massive golden tree-device itself. But it only shows our own reflections. We believe the search can only be initiated by a ruler with the power to genuinely search the world, through authority or other technology, if we are correctly reading the documents we found with it."

"How could the device possibly detect such a thing?"

"We have no idea. This is all highly speculative." Appolonia silently applauded Edward's first genuine admission of skepticism.

"You think it will work for me."

"You rule the empire upon which the sun never sets. If it doesn't work for you, we are at a loss. The tree will run out of fuel. We have no idea how soon, or at what rate of decay, but it seems inevitable."

"Bring us this mirror."

"I have it in a secure place and will bring it. It will take several hours to bring it here. Shall we set a time to reconvene?"

They agreed to meet again the following morning, in the same chamber.

The mirror was large, oval, and otherwise unremarkable. Edward leaned it up against the wall for ease of viewing.

The Queen stared at it. "So far, I see only myself."

Edward pulled out a sheet of notes. "We believe it responds to a linguistic activation code. I've taken the liberty of translating it into Greek, Latin, German, Aryan, and the language of Tibet, and provided a phonetic guide to the pronunciation for each. We are unsure how adaptive it is. The English may suffice."

Appolonia had argued the night before that this piece of information required considerably more caveats. Tell her it is a wild supposition born of Charles' imagination, but reasonable to test given the brief investment of time and energy required to read the words, however absurd they are. Tell her we are at a loss otherwise, having found no other related clue. Edward had nodded then, but said nothing of the kind now.

The Queen read the paper. "Is this some sort of jest?"

Charles stepped forward nervously. "Most of the clues we have followed have been from written records—from history, literature, and folklore. Following the trail of clues, a castle in Germany was, we believe, the source of the more common related fable. A bite of apple followed by stasis—you can see how it attracted our interest."

The Queen sighed, and read the words in a flat, irritated tone: "Mirror, mirror on the wall, who is the fairest of them all?"

The silver surface of the mirror rippled, and a face gradually formed—a young woman of extraordinary beauty. It was some kind of moving pictures device. By her features, the woman could have been European or American, Slavic or Russian. She was white, with brown hair and blue eyes. They all stared, momentarily speechless.

"Who is that?" Appolonia asked.

They all conferred. They had no idea.

After more than a year of searching, they exhausted the most obvious channels. They sketched the woman's face and circulated the sketch through diplomatic and military channels. They posted an advertisement in major newspapers, including the sketch, with contact information so that the woman in question could claim an unexpected inheritance, starting with British papers and slowly ranging out to further and further locales. They determined the relative proportion of the height of her head to its width, and ran searches through Scotland Yard's and Dr. Pyggins' morphic analytic difference engines seeking a match, and identified over fifty likely candidates who were gradually located and eliminated from consideration.

The breakthrough came in 1896, after almost eighteen months of effort. By this point, they had relocated the massive device from Tibet to the Isle of Wight for safekeeping, and Edward was stationed continuously with the device to monitor and protect it, while Appolonia and Charles continued the search.

The device was starting to show signs that time was running out, from Edwards' most recent reports. Its clockwork mechanisms were moving perceptibly more slowly, and two apples had fallen. They agreed to reduce the amount sapped to half a litre per day to try to extend its use.

By now the primary users—scientists trying to unlock the recipe for élan vital to bring the dead or other constructs to life; resurrectionists securing bodies for the medical schools; physicians and surgeons who had discovered numerous medical applications for keeping a limb or wound in stasis, temporarily staying blood loss and the course of infection; and the amorticians who were becoming increasingly popular for their willingness to tamper with a man or woman's bone structure to match what was considered most fashionable—were all willing to absorb a higher cost as supply diminished.

It was June in 1896 when Appolonia finally received a message from a contact at Scotland Yard to come at once, because a man had contacted the police to ask for their help in determining who had placed the inheritance advertisement, suspecting foul play of some kind. They had established Appolonia as the primary contact for the advertisement. anticipating that the woman they sought would be least intimidated by another woman, and because Appolonia had thought Charles incapable of handling the matter with discretion.

After being introduced to him by an officer of the Yard, Appolonia learned, the contact claimed to be private investigator hired by the woman in question. He identified the woman in the sketch as Giselle Verdi, the mistress of the current Camerlengo of the Holy Roman Church, the administrator of the property and revenues of the Holy See. The contact made it clear that running the advertisement in any further Italian newspapers would be considered a diplomatic incident.

Appolonia listened to his explanation in wonder. Once the mirror had shown the woman, she'd been forced to admit that the activation code worked, but she had remained determinedly skeptical that a single unknown woman could be found. It was a needle in a haystack. Impossible.

And now, decidedly possible.

Appolonia begged the contact to arrange an interview for her with Giselle, and offered a substantial reward to both the investigator and Giselle herself, for an hour of her time. The investigator consented, but explained that Giselle had no intention of leaving her home, so the interview would have to occur in the Papal lands.

Appolonia readily agreed, eager to see the woman in the flesh, and regretting only that Charles would insist on chaperoning her on a trip of this length. That would require further chaperones, since she could not travel alone with him—an unmarried man. She initiated the process of hiring a maidservant for herself and two guards.

When they met with Giselle, there could be no question that she was the woman in the mirror. She was breathtaking. Charles felt it necessary to reassure Appolonia that she was Giselle's equal, man of great imagination that he was. She prayed the gesture was not the sort of empty-headed compliment that signaled the beginning of a tiresome and hopeless courtship.

Appolonia had concocted a story to explain why they had been looking for Giselle—that there was an artist in England who had seen her while traveling abroad. An illness rendered him an invalid, and he had become consumed with the desire to paint her before he died. He had pledged his not inconsiderable fortune to anyone who brought her to him, willing to pose for several weeks for a portrait. Assuming his health held long enough to complete the painting, he was certain it would be his masterpiece. Appolonia offered to split the reward with her. The story seemed plausible, and likely to flatter a woman of her obvious beauty.

Giselle indicated that she would need time to consider, and to seek permission from the Camerlengo to travel. Giselle revealed the Camerlengo was not her lover, as commonly assumed, but rather her father.

Appolonia worried that the ire of the Camerlengo, when Giselle failed to return, would be a problem, but they were too close to achieving their goal to stop now. Accidents happened. If he gave her permission to travel, he would be consumed by his own guilt. This was the best course, as opposed to kidnapping her.

The next day, Giselle consented to travel with them, and they set sail for the Isle of Wight.

Appolonia noticed that Charles was becoming increasingly besotted with the girl. This was such a welcome turn of events from her dreaded thought that he had developed some attachment to herself that she encouraged it. She let the two of them speak for hours at a time with only the maid or a guard present.

She should have foreseen the catastrophe that would follow. She would never be able to blame anyone but herself. On the fourth day of the sea voyage, Appolonia found Giselle and Charles dead in Giselle's cabin, having hanged themselves. Giselle's note said they would destroy themselves rather than play a role in the "blasphemous enterprise". Charles' note said that he prayed God would forgive him for tampering in these matters, and that he was determined to protect his angel from misuse.

Appolonia comprehended that Giselle had seduced him and pried out the secret details of the venture. He had been so proud of his discoveries, and she was so beautiful. And he was a man of faith, and her the daughter of the Camerlengo on her way to being fed to a machine.

It was a disastrous turn of events.

Appolonia quickly fetched their supply of vitaldehyde and gave Giselle's body a sufficient dose to preserve her beauty as fresh as if she were still alive, at least until they arrived at the Isle and could acquire more. She would have to stop in London and verify with the Queen whether a dead but preserved beauty was still the most beautiful woman in the world. If Giselle's body represented tainted or inappropriate fuel now, there was no telling what placing her in a pod would do. She had not eaten of the apple. Appolonia sliced a piece off and wedged it into her throat, but feared that this was entirely too irregular.

Charles had made no arrangements for the disposition of his share in the untimely event of his death. She supposed she and Edward would simply divide it. When she arrived on British soil, she telegraphed Edward to join her.

The Queen heard the news of Charles and Giselle's deaths calmly.

Edward cursed the setback, and noted that he had an exciting development to report.

"Let's have your good news first before we go any further," Appolonia suggested. "I am weary of bad news."

The Queen concurred. "Yes, let's hear any further findings before we go on."

Edward nodded. "I have been studying the device closely over the last year on the Isle, trying to discern its true purpose. We ascertained that it required the beautiful as fuel, but to what end? The sap that we so prize appears to be a by-product, rather than an end in and of itself.

"I asked myself--why would an advanced race, and one that was dying, build a machine to store the most beautiful members of another race? I could only conclude it was something they wished they had done for themselves, in the sunset years of their evolution. Why would they wish for beautiful women from the earliest days of their history through to the present? It could simply be a kind of museum—an homage to what they had been, and a warehouse for study. But, surely their primary focus at the time was on what they would have done, had they had the foresight, to preserve their dying race.

"Why does any race die out? Things evolve past the point of usefulness. Features that were once assets become unusable. I concluded that they wanted beautiful women from their past to refresh their lines, as breeding stock, to re-vitalize themselves, and recover some traits from their past that had been lost. It is a device not for individual immortality but for the immortality of the race."

Appolonia stared at Edward in astonishment. "Can it be? That would be extraordinary. But the women are in stasis. They could no more conceive than bleed or breathe."

Edward nodded. "I decided to run an experiment. I took a woman—I think Helen herself—out of her pod."

"You should have told us," Appolonia charged, unable to hold her tongue. "This experiment of yours might explain the decreased vitality of the device even more than our failure to find the next sacrifice." Did he understand nothing about experimental controls?

"It was necessary. I did not want to send us all down this chain of reason if it proved foolish, and detract from the necessary work of finding the woman in the mirror. But I can report that after one month, Helen's body showed signs of returning to use. She was warmer, and I could hear her blood circulating. Within two months, she was still like a woman in a coma, but I judged her body ready for the experiment, and attempted to impregnate her. After six months, I could detect the signs of pregnancy. She has never woken up, but the pregnancy continues. Within a month, we will be able to see if she can deliver the child, and what such a child is like."

The Queen rose to her feet. "We at least should have been informed." She began to pace. "I will return with the mirror. The necessity of keeping the machine functional is all the greater, given these revelations."

They waited.

Appolonia looked at Edward in disgust. "What made you think you were worthy, assuming it was the right thing to do, to breed with that glorious woman for whom so many warred?"

The Queen returned with a large contingent of guards, who fell upon them and restrained them.
"We have wondered at the wisdom of allowing you to control the production of this vital resource. We tried to balance secrecy and necessity. Now that the device is safely on British soil, and you have discovered as much as you have, it is past time that the government seized control of this device.

"I knew the woman had died the day she killed herself, for on that morning the mirror showed me another face. Appolonia, you'll be pleased to know that you, at least, will continue to have a role in this enterprise, though not one I think that you would have chosen for yourself."

She gave a signal and the guards executed Edward.

Appolonia sobbed. "You can't! After all we've done."

The Queen had the guards continue to restrain her. One guard pried her mouth open, as the wicked Queen shoved a slice of apple between her teeth.

Mae Empson began selling fantasy and horror short fiction to magazines and anthologies in July 2010. Publications include stories in the anthologies *Cthulhurotica*, *In Situ*, *Historical Lovecraft*, and *Steam Works*. She is a member of the Horror Writers Association, and of HorrorPNW—the Pacific Northwest chapter of HWA. She lives in Seattle, WA. She has a Master's degree in English literature from Indiana University at Bloomington, and graduated with honors in English and in Creative Writing from the University of North Carolina at Chapel Hill, where she received the Robert B. House Memorial Prize in Poetry in 1995. Read Mae's blog at http://maeempson.wordpress.com

How to Hack Your Dragon
By Christine Danse

I don't believe in God, I believe in us.
Eddie Izzard

After the smoke haze cleared and all the partygoers had gone, he led her down the darkened street toward the stable. She laughed as he wove.

"I warned you not to hack your mets," she said. "You're going to give yourself alcohol poisoning."

He ignored her gentle reprimand. "You're gonna love her. You're gonna love her," he repeated, over and over again.

"I'm sure I will. Hold on." She grabbed his upper arm as he careened toward a mailbox.

With a toothy grin, he stumbled into her and encircled her waist. "You're gonna love her," he breathed into her ear.

Salome squealed with laughter and pushed away. "*Stop* that! I'm sure I will, if you stop slobbering on me, you beast." She bared her delicate fangs in irony. Travis had reloaded his original human genome three years ago and hadn't added a single thero mod since. Though she adored his hazel eyes and cropped sandy hair, she sometimes missed his shaggy wolf tail and the ears that tickled her thighs when he nibbled her down there.

At ten stories high, the stable loomed shoulders above the sleeping houses. Square landing platforms spiked its upper stories, each like a concrete tongue under a shuttered aerie entrance. Inside the ground level foyer were the familiar smells of animal musk and earthy dung, straw and brimstone.

"Where you going?" asked Travis, as Salome reached for a door to the right of the entry. She looked over her shoulder at him, one graceful leg poised mid-step. He admired the rounded calf and slender ankle as he added, "I've moved up in the world." He chucked his head toward the elevator and offered her his elbow.

She took it. "What happened to Pearl?"

"I traded her in." He avoided looking at her. Salome had been fond of his doe-eyed kirin.

They rode the elevator to the eighth floor in silence. The hallway they stepped into was empty and quiet, save for the muffled groans of a restless mount. Feather particles and glittering shed scales dusted the floor.

He led her to a door near the end of the hall and pressed his thumb to a security pad. The door opened to a long room. Cubbies, mostly empty, lined the walls, and black leather tack hung from an industrial-sized hook. Against the right wall gaped the dark, square window of a stable stall. Its chest-high door was closed and locked. Farther on, the long room ended in a pair of closed double doors—the flight entrance

"A private aerie?" Salome asked, looking about.

Travis grinned. "They're all private. You should know that. Oh! You don't *fly*. You've been old enough for two years, so sometimes I *forget*."

Her ears flattened to her skull and she smacked him across the shoulder. "I'm afraid of heights."

"Typical cat." He laughed and ducked her next swing fluidly.

At the sound of their voices, a large, dark head stretched from the stable, its muzzle long and tapered.

"Oh," said Salome. She stepped forward and stared for a long while at the creature in the stall, grooming her catgirl tail idly. One slender tortoiseshell ear turned back. "Just a basic mount? You couldn't buy yourself something better for your 25th birthday?"

Travis smiled indulgently. "Nothing basic about her when I get done."

"She's going to take a lot of work," said Salome. The dragon on the other side of the door stared at them blandly--a standard build with sooty grey hide and two short horns like a goat's. It blinked its wet black eyes and whuffled at Travis's shirt sleeve, recognizing its new owner by the scent that had been hardwired into its memory, then lifted its ridged nose and snuffled curiously at the air in front of Salome. Its breath was surprisingly cool, and Salome raised a hand to feel it. "Not even a fire breather?"

Travis hung on the door and draped an arm over the serpentine neck. "What, are we going to war?"

"Har har," said Salome, with a sideways look. "Intelligence level?"

"Three-year-old."

She snorted. "Could you have gotten her any dumber? Don't answer that. Well, you're going to have to do a lot with this one to impress me." She patted the smooth hide of its neck. "Are you going to add scales?"

"Nope." At her dubious look, he added, "Plenty of dragons don't have scales. And be prepared to be impressed. The dragon you see before you now is not the dragon you will see in a few days. She'll be able to outsmart a seven-year-old, and you'll see why I ordered smooth hide."

The dragon sought with a long black tongue for Salome's hand. Nose wrinkling, she pulled it from reach. "It's one thing to hack your dog to act like a cat. Where do you plan to find the code to jack up its intelligence? You don't plan to write it yourself, do you? You'll be in very big trouble if you uplift her."

Travis placed a finger aside his nose and jabbed upward with his thumb. "Neighbor's got a new Celarus Gryphon. Latest brain build. If the thing had fingers, you could teach it to play chess. But perfectly legal intelligence."

Salome arched one carefully shaped eyebrow. "...which you won't be obtaining legally," she added, dryly. "Blood sample?"

"Hell, no! Thing would bite my arm off. And its aerie is locked. I've got a different plan."

"And just what is your plan?"

Travis, leaning heavily on the wall, smiled. "How am I supposed to impress you if I tell you my secret?"

Salome flicked a dried fleck of yogurt from her tail. "Right. No plan, just as I thought."

"I have one," he protested.

She reached forward to scritch between the dragon's horns. It hummed and pushed into her hand. "I'll give you one week."

"One week," agreed Travis. He snagged her waist and licked the paper-thin edge of her ear. "You won't be disappointed."

At the sound of the door opening, Edward the dog jumped from the couch's backrest to rub his lean side against Travis's leg. The apartment was in a pleasant state of ruin; yogurt jars and empty alcohol bottles littered the tables and spilled onto the floor. The party had been homegrown. Travis cultured the yogurts, and Salome brought the alcohol, a type made from a yeast strain she'd developed as a birthday gift for Travis. He was still under the effects of that now. Traces of a designer herb still lingered in the air, another birthday gift.

The initial uplifting buzz from the alcohol wore off, leaving Travis' brain a muddled sludge. He rooted through the fridge, pawing aside yogurt jars with scribbled labels until he found one with the letters "ETOH-METS." He spooned it into his mouth straight from the jar. In minutes, his mind cleared as the metabolizers in the yogurt chewed up the alcohol streaming through his veins.

At his feet, Edward mewed for water. "Good boy," he said, stroking the dog's head as he spilled water into the bowl near the pantry. Edward crouched to his elbows and lapped daintily.

Travis kicked aside jars on the way to his office. The clock inside read three in the morning, but he couldn't go to bed just yet. His mind spun with project ideas. He dropped into his desk chair. "The Beast," his seven-year-old bacterial CPU, glowed beneath his hands. The bacterial colony lay beneath a plate of glass half an inch thick; it doubled as his desktop.

The bioluminescence of the bacteria was his doing, one of his first really successful hacks. In hibernation, the CPU glowed dully, but at his touch, flickers of will-o'-the-wisp light chased themselves around the desktop. The screen above came to life, opening to his last window: a three dimensional diagram of an abstract shape, spinning slowly. The model of a virus.

Viruses were the favorite of hackers, who often employed them to do what viruses naturally did best: act as microbial cuckoos to lay their rogue genetic data inside a host cell's nucleus. Infecting bacterial CPUs was their major use, though their application had broadened over the years. A clever hacker could theoretically plant code in any living entity.

Or, mused Travis, *pluck* code from any living entity.

Travis had programmed more than his share of viruses, though he had never accomplished what he was attempting now: to develop a virus that stole snippets of DNA from cells. If he could secure a patent on a virus that retrieved code, he'd make millions. But the design had to pass his first test—to steal copies of the newly-developed intelligence genes from his neighbor's Celarus.

He only intended to tweak the code a bit before crashing—he'd finish the thing tomorrow—but soon the early morning sun was peeking through the blinds and he had a slim vial of virus sitting on his desk, fresh from the generator.

The clock read seven. If he hurried down to the stable, he'd be able to catch his neighbor exercising the gryphon on the lawn. "Exercise," of course, meaning "to strut the beast around in public so the entire neighborhood could admire this latest expensive toy." It posed a perfect opportunity for Travis to come innocently in contact with the gryphon and steal a bit of code right out from underneath his neighbor's nose—smiling all the while. He hadn't planned on trying the virus until tomorrow, but the slats of morning sunlight urged him up.

Travis showered last night's film of sweat and smoke from his body, tossed back a Liquid Sleep, and threw a can of dog food down for Edward. He struggled for a minute with how to administer the virus to the gryphon; his thoughts looped like a skipping vinyl until the Liquid Sleep kicked in. He settled for coating his left hand with the virus solution and slipping it into the clean pocket of his hoodie. Into the other pocket, he stuffed a clean tissue.

The morning was bright and brisk. Travis found the gryphon lying on the grass in front of the stable, enjoying the light of the early sun, which gleamed over its tawny hide and highlighted the curves of its muscles. Travis' neighbor, Horner, stood in the shade nearby, scrolling through something on his hand pad.

"How does the market look?" asked Travis, strolling up with his hands stuffed casually into his pockets. The gryphon gave him a long look through a half-hooded yellow eye. The massive talon it had stretched on the grass flexed slowly, claws like scythes bending the green blades.

Horner smiled a neighborly smile. "Hey there, Trav. Looking okay. Celarus is up one percent, but BIOP's gone down."

"That's too bad," clucked Travis.

Travis' neighbor was a biotech investor by trade, a family tradition began by Horner Senior. "My father recognized the trend before anyone else," Horner often boasted. Then, in an attempt at modesty, he would add, "Of course, tech could have gone the electronics route. He was lucky." His father's "luck" ensured Horner a comfortable childhood—and now an endless parade of bioengineered trophies.

Travis nodded toward the gryphon. "That's a really nice mount you have there. New Celarus, huh?"

"Yes, sir. New HI-INT technology. You familiar?"

"Just a rumor in a 'zine a few months back. Wasn't sure if it was real. It's out already?" The Liquid Sleep hit his system finally. It filled his limbs with a fluid energy, making his arms buoyant and his hands itchy. He curled his fingers inside the hoodie pockets, balling and unballing the tissue.

Horner smiled like a salesman. "It's real, and it's out. Very exclusive, though. Have to have good standing with the distributor."

Or wave a credit the size of your ego at them, thought Travis, as he smiled. Out loud, he whistled long and low. "Wow. Well, she's a beauty. Mind if I pet her? Does she like that?"

"Yeah, sure, go ahead." Horner crouched to the gryphon's side. "Hey, baby. This is a friend of mine. He thinks you're the most beautiful thing on this earth, and he's just going to give you a little pet." He looked up at Travis. "She's seen that we've been talking pleasantly and that I accept you, so she should, too." He scritched below the gryphon's chin. The feather-tufted tail twitched once in the grass before settling.

Save me the theatrics. "A bit like my kirin." Travis approached at a crouch, as if making an impression on a small child. "Hey there, pretty girl," he crooned, stretching his left hand toward the wicked curved beak, his skin shining dully with dried virus solution. The gryphon watched him levelly and allowed him to pet the soft feathers of its brow. "You're soft." He stroked the feathers for a long moment, brushing his palm over the nearby nares and thoroughly inoculating the beast. Standing, he returned his hands casually to his pockets. "Very mild-mannered. What a beauty. So how does the HI-INT technology work? Is it an implant? Cell surgery? Or a gene?"

"No, it's a gene. Celarus preloads its gryphons and dragons with it at the breeder, but they're trying to get a mod on the market. They're testing how well it works on mature brains. But I tell you it won't work. Mount needs to grow with it."

"Hm," grunted Travis. *Elitist,* he thought. "I wonder why you think that is? Something with the way the brain develops physically?"

"Not just physically. Developmentally. I can't imagine taking something that's developed with the intelligence of a dog and suddenly elevating it to the level of a child. Traumatizing and dangerous. Needs to develop that way." He went on to cite examples of cases gone awry.

Travis nodded with feigned interest while he kept one eye on the gryphon. He was biding his time. The virus was a quick-acting one, and the histamine-releaser he'd added to the solution would have an effect any moment. The gryphon, once calm, now switched its tail and dragged its claws through the grass. Its blinking grew more frequent.

"Good to know," said Travis. "I was planning on getting a new mount today. My first flyer. Just got my flying license last week. Turned 25 yesterday."

"Congratulations!"

"Thanks. Yeah, it's either gonna be a dragon or a gryphon. I think I'll go for the HI-INT. Why wait for a mod? I think you're right."

The gryphon groaned quietly and rustled its wings. Travis noted the glint of mucus under one nare. Perfect. Now, he just needed to get into firing range. "Aw, what's the matter, baby?" he cooed, stepping forward to pet it. "Too much tech talk for you?" The eyes were definitely watering now. His neighbor stood by, smiling, oblivious of the volcano that was about to explode.

The gryphon groaned again, louder this time. It recoiled its head, and—with violent suddenness—sneezed on Travis. A spray of mucus covered him from head to knees.

The gryphon sprang to its feet and sneezed again—once, twice—while Travis spread his arms, pretending to be stunned. Part of his expression wasn't an act; he was covered with far more mucus than he'd expected.

With a cry of dismay, Horner jumped forward. "I am *so sorry*. Here, let me help you."

"No, no. It's okay. I've got it." Travis wiped his face with the clean tissue he'd stowed in his pocket. "I'll just...go upstairs and change. It's no big deal." He left bearing a sheen of mucus. The gryphon was rubbing its beak miserably in the grass. Travis felt vaguely sorry for it, though the effect wouldn't last long. The worst of it would be gone in just a few minutes. Hopefully, Horner would forget the episode ever happened.

On his way back to the apartment, Travis stopped at the mailbox. He found a package inside, a small padded envelope with a bump at one end. "Fragile," said its red stamped letters. He tore the end from the envelope and pulled out a small vial. It read "Octoflauge-M." The camo mod he'd ordered—at last! A shiver of excitement powered him up the stairs.

In his office, he scraped the mucus from his shirt and dropped a glob into the CPU's receiver to scan. As the bases scrolled across the screen, he unfolded a piece of paper from the envelope:

BIOP Octoflauge-M Mountmod Information
WARNING: Not for use in humans or non-rideable pets.

Congratulations on purchasing the BIOP Octoflauge-M mountmod. For superior camouflage action, please follow these quick-start instructions. **Code source:** Octopoda spp., Bradypodion taeniabronchum

Travis glanced through the instructions--eyes skimming over the words "chromatophores" and "skin texture"—before tossing them to the side. He took a chug from the yerba mate power drink Salome had left in his fridge. The Liquid Sleep didn't have the effect it used to on him. The edgy energy barely kept him awake.

"Come on, babies," he urged the CPU, watching the code unfurl. When the first non-viral genes appeared, he crowed. Genes for wings, behavior, sight. His virus had snagged the gryphon's code.

Once the gryphon genome was loaded onto the computer, isolating the HI-INT code was easier than he'd expected. Parts of it were similar to older intelligence genes— child's play to spot. The code had been dispersed as a series of small genes over five different chromosomes, but he had them all isolated by noon. The real trick was weaving them with the Octoflauge mod into the dragon's genome. It took a sharp eye and a working knowledge of brain coding to fit the pieces together without programming the dragon's brain into a pile of goo. He had the knowledge, but his sharp eyes were blurred. He squeezed the bridge of nose between his eyes to keep his vision focused on the screen.

Before the sun's light disappeared from his window, he had the new dragon genome loaded into the code for a carrier virus. Whispering, "Let's impress Salome," he clicked "execute" and let the generator do its magic.

The dragon hung its head over the stall door, waiting for Travis. It had apparently learned to associate him with food, for it licked its muzzle and watched him intently as he approached, its eyes traveling to his hands and pockets.

Travis chuckled. "Soon, you'll be telling me which flavor you'd like." He pulled a salmon cube from a bag in his pocket. The block shone with a thin coat of virus slime, but the dragon—obviously not picky—whuffled and sucked it from his hand. Travis smiled and patted it on the nose. "Good girl."

The dragon smacked its jaw, looking for more treats. Its black eyes shone with a greedy cleverness.

"You're smart when you're hungry," mused Travis. "Maybe you don't need this mod, after all. Maybe if I just keep you hungry I'll keep you on your toes." As he spoke, he patted his pockets and held up his empty hands. "See? Nothing more here."

The dragon dropped to its haunches and rested its chin atop the stall door. It settled and sighed, eyes tracking Travis, who lowered to the floor nearby.

The cold concrete felt divine underneath him, as if he could just melt into its pores. "I know, I know," he said to the dragon, leaning back. "I haven't taken you out yet. Don't worry. I'm itching to be in the air, too. Just sleep a little, will you? You'll need it."

But the dragon didn't sleep. It watched Travis quietly as the hacker fidgeted with a piece of heavy leather tack and tugged on all of the straps, testing their strength. A little time passed before the dragon began to moan, softly. Travis looked up. Strings of mucus stretched from the dragon's nose to the ground, trembling with each of its breaths. The dragon gave him a miserable look and then withdrew its head with a grunt. From inside the stall came the sound of a heavy flop. The floor beneath Travis shook.

Travis leaped to his feet, teetered as the blood rushed to his head, and peered inside. The dragon was on its side, breathing heavily. It opened one watery eye to peer at him dully, then closed it again with a snort that propelled a spray of snot against the wall.

Quietly, Travis entered the stall and crouched beside the dragon in the straw. He caressed his knuckles over the skin beneath its eye, wetting his fingers with tears. "Good girl. You've just got a cold. It's just a normal reaction. It'll pass."

As if expressing disagreement, the dragon let out a shuddering groan and a whuff. Travis chuckled and stroked its side until its breathing settled into the rhythm of sleep—steady and deep, entrancing.

"There you go. Good idea," he whispered. He relaxed against the back wall of the stall and closed his eyes, following the sounds of rise and fall. The aerie's smells of dragon musk and leather wrapped him up like a cozy blanket. "Good idea…"

When Travis opened his eyes, the dragon was gone. He thought his bleary vision was playing tricks on him, but when he blinked and stretched his eyes open again, the stall was empty. With a dizzy rush, he shot to his feet. He glanced at his watch. Almost two hours had passed.

The stall door was closed and intact, the stable peaceful. Empty.

Travis pressed the heel of his hand between his eyes. He couldn't seem to focus them properly. With blurred vision and a head still thick with sleep, he stumbled to the stall door. Had the dragon—with heightened intelligence—opened it and left?

He fumbled open the stall door's latch and took one step out, regarding the vacant aerie with dismay—but only for a moment. With a sudden sound of popping and scraping, a huge form blasted past him. His hands gripped the edge of the door reflexively, and he found himself holding on as it sailed open with a crash. His legs scissored in the air—for a moment, weightless.

His feet hit the floor. The air rippled and the room was filled with the sound of rustling. His vision blurred and cleared in turns. No, not his vision—the room itself.

An invisible force crashed into one wall of cubbies, sending a rain of bottles and tins bouncing through the air. The dragon's illusion was broken by its rapid movement down the length of the room, concrete blurring into smooth hide. It sped toward the closed double doors of the flight entrance, its tail lashing behind it like a whip. Color returned to it from the head down, as if grey paint had been spilled on its crown and ran down its neck and sides, leaving only concrete-colored legs and wing tips. Travis marveled at the speed of the change. The effect was dramatic; while still, the dragon had been as good as invisible.

When the dragon lowered its head and flattened its wings to its sides, Travis realized it planned to ram the flight doors open. It would crush itself to a pulp if it tried. He vaulted toward the wall panel, pressing his thumb against the security pad. The doors slid open, revealing late afternoon sunlight and the tops of trees just before the dragon blotted them from view. It leapt.

Travis let out a cry and sprinted to the edge of the landing platform. He stumbled to a short stop, arms windmilling, a hair's-breadth from a three-story free-fall. For a split moment, the dragon hung in the air before him. It spread massive webbed wings, membranes glowing red in the light of the sun. And then it crashed to the grass below, the motion of the wings reflecting the frantic flapping of Travis's arms.

With a sorrowful cry, the dragon flung back its head and faded from sight against the lawn.

"*Shit.*" Mounts were imprinted with the ability to fly. He thought he'd been careful not to affect those codes. But that's probably what he got for installing two brain-affecting modifications at the same time—on no sleep.

The air wavered and the dragon flickered in and out of view. Travis caught an occasional glimpse of its shadow stretching and shrinking over the lawn. Leaves and grass flew like confetti in its wake, leading rapidly to the edge of the building.

A narrow flight of steps led down from the flight pad. He took them two at a time. "Dragon!" he cried. "Stop!" Lungs already burning, he fumbled through his pocket and withdrew a salmon cube, partially smashed. He fell against the wall, chest heaving.

A whuffle and stirring of wings, and the dragon reappeared, neck stretched toward him.

"There you are," he panted. When he extended his hand with the cube, the dragon withdrew and looked at him. He forced a reassuring smile, and it resumed its cautious inspection of his palm, unfurling its black tongue and hooking the cube. As it chewed, Travis took its dangling reins. Morsel swallowed, the dragon sat and licked its lips clean.

"Well, the Octoflauge worked," said Travis, dryly. "And you aren't so dumb and docile anymore, huh? Now we just need to teach you some trust." He extended his hand again.

The dragon sniffed it, then fixed him with a look when it found no treat. But it let him pet its muzzle, and even made a humming sound when he knuckled the underside of its strong jaw.

"There you go. Just like that." He massaged its neck, and soon it lay down. "Just... like... that," he soothed, as its eyes slowly shuttered. "Now, let's get you back to the stable and I'll run a bio on you to see what's wrong."

Travis tugged lightly on the reins, but the dragon lay bonelessly on the ground. "All right, baby. Up!" He tickled the mount's belly. With a shiver and grunt, it rolled to all fours and followed Travis to the front of the stable, where the large, dragon-sized front door opened with a press of the hacker's thumb.

In his head, Travis listed the diagnostics he would need to run. A full brain and nerve scan, certainly, and a scan of the dragon's genome for broken code. The HI-INT genes, the Octoflauge control center—he might have overwritten the flight code with either of these. And what else had he screwed up?

Travis hurried forward—and was pulled to a sudden stop as the reins went taut. Behind him sat the dragon, balking.

The dragon yanked against the reins. "Hey!" Travis yelped, tightening his hold. He watched the mount's neck veins bulge with strain. He gritted his teeth and braced his legs, leaning back for more pull. "Come... on..."

"Having trouble?"

Travis looked up to find his neighbor grinning at him. "Perfectly fine," he grunted.

Sensing slack in the reins, the dragon pulled back sharply, jerking them from Travis's hands.

"No! No! No!" he yelled, scrambling to grab them. His fingers clenched around leather, and he pulled tight. The dragon cried out, rearing and bucking. Flapping wings kicked a cloud of dirt into Travis's eyes.

Horner shielded his face with one hand. "A smart model, huh?"

"Yeah," he grunted. "Took—your—advice."

Horner crossed his arms and watched the struggle calmly. "Huh. Funny that she's giving you so much trouble. Did you make sure to load the security debug?"

"Security debug?" Travis blinked painfully, grit scratching his eyes. Tears trailed down his cheeks.

"Yeah. The distributor should have given you a debugger to load. Inserts a gene that shuts off the fear code." His grin widened. "You're in a load of shit if the dealer forgot to tell you about it. It makes the mounts spook at the sight of their own shadows. Makes 'em useless for flight—they're scared of heights. An antitheft bug to prevent mod ripping. Here." He offered Travis a short grey stick. An emergency tranq pen, procured from the lock box near the door of the stable.

"Thanks," deadpanned Travis, taking it.

With the tip of an invisible hat, his neighbor smiled and strode away.

"Okay, dragon. Let's get this over with." He looped the reins around his hand as he approached, holding the lines taut. The dragon spread wings to full length, a defensive display. Travis could see the whites of its eyes. He lifted the pen to his teeth and spat its cap to the lawn. "Hold... still..." Clenching the reins with one hand, he plunged the pen into the dragon's shoulder.

The dragon screeched, arms flinging. One elbow clubbed Travis in the chest and lifted him off the ground. He sailed through the air.

Travis lay on the grass where he landed, staring up at a sky gone impossibly orange. Nearby, the dragon swayed and sagged to the ground. For a minute, he listened to its piteous whimpers and ignored the startled stares of a woman and her daughter. He lifted two fingers to his temples. Pressing the skin, he croaked, *"Contact number one."*

Salome answered his call after three rings. "Yeah?"

He could hear her trance music playing in the background. She must be working. He'd interrupted her groove.

Travis released a sigh like a punctured gasbag. "Help me."

"Well," said Salome fifteen minutes later, staring at the drugged dragon. Its backside had disappeared against the lawn, and the green, spiked camo crept all the way up its spine, giving the beast a ridge of grass. "I'm impressed."

Travis looked up at her. She'd pulled her riding jacket over her work-at-home camisole and yoga pants; he noted the way the soft cotton of the pants accentuated her curves. "Really?" he asked, ignoring a curious look from her racer, Streak. The ostrosaur was the fastest thing that ran on the ground—the ideal mount for a speedster afraid of flying. Salome had put a lot of custom work into it. Tonight, its feathers were iridescent black and flecked with white, like a starling's.

She nodded. "Yeah, really. *Very* impressed. I think this is the most trouble you've gotten yourself into yet. Dare I even ask what happened?"

"HI-INT came with a security bug," he said, accepting her hand up. "Everything except salmon cubes scare her into fits."

She regarded the dragon. "Doesn't look very scared to me. Just drugged."

He swiped his face with his shirtsleeve. "Emergency tranq. We have about an hour and forty before she snaps out of it."

"Of course, you want me to watch her. No, don't kiss me! Go—go do what you need to do before she snaps out of it."

Travis stole a quick peck on her cheek. Her fading voice followed him down the street; she urged the dragon to stand and walk to the side of the building, where they would be less likely to attract attention. Based on her tone, the entreaties were not very effective.

By the time Travis reached the apartment, he'd convinced himself he would need to reboot the dragon's genome and start all over again. Of course, his neighbor would have already loaded the security debugger onto his gryphon, so it would be a part of the gryphon's genome—he just hadn't known to look for it the first go around. This meant Travis would have to get a fresh sample from the gryphon, which was now stabled and out of his reach for the night. He would have to reboot the dragon for now, then come up with a novel way to nab the gryphon genome— again. He wouldn't risk his neighbor's suspicion by trying the sneezing trick a second time.

But he needn't have worried. As he reached for the vial of Octoflauge—he may as well at least include *that* mod while rebooting—he noticed the bottle next to it and remembered that he had set aside some of his original gryphon sample. He was so tired and muddle-brained that he'd forgotten. "Oh, thank you," he breathed, flopping into the desk chair.

He uncapped the vial, spilled the last blob of mucus into the receiver, and watched the code scroll past as he tossed back another Liquid Sleep. The bases blurred together—not because of any illusion this time, but because of bleary eyes. He recognized the code for many things, including the HI-INT genes. They seemed so painfully obvious to him now. But then, they needn't be so hidden, need they? They had a bug to protect them from people like Travis.

An hour passed. He paused the stream of code three times to pace up and down the hall and splash water onto his face. He saw nothing but standard gryphon genes, virus code, and nonsense that wasn't code for anything. The last feeble rays of light died away. He imagined Salome entertaining a twitchy racer and a drunk dragon. He called her.

"She's still down," said Salome. "How's your progress?"

"What progress? I'm still working on—Wait. Call you back." He paused the code and scrolled back. There it was—a strange little bit of code at the end of one chromosome, nestled amongst a string of nonsense bases so that it seemed like nonsense itself. He isolated it and ran it through the simulator, and sure enough, it seemed to be a switch for another gene—one that was nestled in the code for HI-INT.

"Well, hello…" He'd found his debugger.

The actual work took little time—isolating, splicing, fabricating the virus, running the job through the generator. Within twenty minutes, he had a new vial in hand. *"Incoming call,"* purred his earpiece as he stood to rescue his girlfriend and dragon. *"Salome,"* it added.

"Receive call. Hi, I'm leaving now. I found it."

"It disappeared."

"It—what? What disappeared?" He leaned on the doorjamb and pressed the heel of his hand between his eyes.

Her voice was dry with irritation. "Your dragon. She just woke up and disappeared."

He breathed a curse. "Hold on."

Full dark had fallen. Travis jogged haltingly to the stable and found Salome standing at its side under the wan light of a street lamp, petting the muzzle of her nervous racer. His gaze traveled over the stable lawn, but he saw no dragon.

Travis opened the bag of salmon cubes he'd brought and shook two onto his hand. "Here, dragon…" he called.

"That's half your problem there—you still haven't named her yet."

"Ssh ssh ssh," hushed Travis, with a flap of his hand, but the night remained still. No strange movement, no shadows under the streetlights.

Salome stroked her racer's neck. "I think she's gone. She just suddenly came to. Rolled onto her feet, saw us, squealed, and disappeared. Spooked the shit out of Streak."

"Did you see which direction she went?"

"Babe. She was invisible."

"Camouflaged," he corrected. "The mod's based on octopus and chameleon genes. You didn't see any trees or grass moving? Hear her crashing through the neighborhood?"

"I was focusing on keeping Streak from bolting. No sense losing both of our mounts, now, is there?"

He closed his eyes. He just needed to be able to think. A soft, nervous sound from Streak distracted him. Opening his eyes, he regarded the racer's slender face. "I wonder if you still sense her, huh?" The question sparked a thought. He stood suddenly straighter. "Hey. Salome, do you think you'd be able to track her by smell?"

"No. Don't you remember? I had the sound and smell mods downgraded." She tapped her petite, human nose.

Travis did remember now. The heightened senses had been too intense for her. When he still had his wolf mods three years ago, he'd found them exhilarating. He'd been able to smell and hear everything—everything from what his professors ate for lunch to what women really talked about in the bathroom. It was a fun outfit he'd worn for five years, but he eventually found it old, and the world didn't take you as seriously when you had a tail sticking out of your jeans and ears the size of hands. Sometimes he missed it. He still kept the bottle of leftover wolf mods in his office, in case one day—

He snapped his fingers and pushed off from the wall. "Stable Streak and come to the apartment with me. I've got a plan."

"Wait. What? Is this anything like your plan to upgrade your dragon?"

"No. Better."

Salome sat on the office couch with a pillow cushion on her face. "This is ridiculous. Why don't you tell me what you're doing?"

Travis hunched over his computer. "Because you'd probably yell at me and tell me how to do what I'm doing better."

A grunt. "And your problem with that is...?"

"I love you," he sing-songed. He turned up the music ever so slightly, hoping it would drown out the soft sounds of the generator working. He stole a look at his girlfriend as it processed. She reclined with her smooth knees slightly bent and her arms draped back over the armrest, a square pillow where her face should be, brown hair spilling out from underneath. Her tail twitched with lazy impatience.

He cleared his throat noisily as the generator beeped with completion. "Gotta run to the bathroom," he said as he slipped the small vial from the generator and closed out the programs he'd been using, eliminating all immediate traces of his work in case Salome got curious. It wouldn't matter in a few minutes, anyway, but he didn't want to ruin the surprise—not this one.

Over the little bathroom sink, he tapped out the contents of the vial and rubbed them into his nose. It smelled like the slick dampness of gelatin and the leather that still clung to his fingers.

He looked into the mirror, memorizing the color of his hazel eyes and the pink curves of his ears. It might be a while before he saw them again.

At first, he didn't feel anything—just the heavy, dull feeling of a body pushed past the limits of exhaustion. And then he was blinking back tears and clearing his throat before he realized it had hit him. Sneezing violently, he fumbled for the roll of toilet paper.

The pain, when it started, punched him in the gut. With a muffled groan, he squatted to the ground and rolled into a ball on the cold tile floor. The pain snaked up to his ears and exploded his toes and tailbone. It stretched his feet and pulled his nose. If he could suck a breath in through a thick clog of mucus, he would have screamed.

The change twisted Travis cruelly—far faster and more intense than any he'd experienced. In a little corner of his mind, he reflected that he had done a good job with hacking the code that would speed up the process. Maybe too good. He worried his anatomy would not be able to take the rapid transformation, and he'd die an agonizing death on the cold bathroom floor, only a dozen feet from his unsuspecting girlfriend.

Salome banged on the door. The sound exploded in his ears. "Travis?" she boomed. "What's going on? Did you fall in?"

He made a strangled mewling sound, then gave up. He might have asked her to call an ambulance. He wondered how the paramedics would treat him when they got there, how loudly they'd shout into his ears, how roughly they'd shake his tight shoulders. How many times would they shove the smelling salts under his nose before tossing him onto a stretcher and shipping him, writhing, to the ER?

And then the pain abated as quickly as it had come. He pushed up onto his elbows and blew his nose into a wad of toilet paper until the smells of the bathroom rushed in: toilet water, soap, mildew.

"I'm fine, I'm fine," he rasped.

"Are you all right? You sound like—"

He opened the door. Salome stared at him, mouth open mid-sentence.

"—shit," she finished.

He glanced back into the mirror to see what she saw: ears stretched grey and triangular, nose pulled straight and tipped with black, eyes golden. He didn't realize how badly he'd missed the wolf outfit until he met the wild eyes of his reflection. He bared long teeth at Salome and said, "Surprise."

She punched his shoulder. "*This* was your plan?"

"Why? Are you going to yell at me and tell me how to do it better?"

"No," she said, leaning in suddenly to lick his bottom lip. The smell of her filled his nostrils—rosewater and hair oil and ginger salad dressing. "But I might toss you on the ground and ravish you."

"I might just take you up on that—*after* I find my dragon." When he stumbled a step in the hall, he added, "And sleep."

They walked down to the stable much like the night before, save Travis was drunk on exhaustion instead of modified alcohol, and the world was alive to him: the smell of asphalt and grass, people and mounts. The sounds of motors running and children laughing in the neighborhood park, of muffled conversations and mailbirds hooting. All the sensations of teeming urban civilization.

An old woman walking her lapfox glared at them as they walked by—beastpunks, freaks. Travis flashed her an extra-toothy smile, feeling 19 again. Salome, catching the expression and the woman's glare, grinned and pinched him on the ass, just at the base of his swishing tail. His yelp excited the lapfox into a flurry of yipping. The woman let out an indignant cry as it strained at the leash.

Travis and Salome stifled their laughter all the way down the street. When the stable driveway was in sight, Salome cuffed him on the shoulder and reminded him to be serious.

"Serious? You started it. I—" He stopped.

Salome watched him keenly. "You smell her?"

He nodded. "Yeah." He led them over the expanse of stable lawn. Their feet kicked up the sharp smell of crushed grass; he ignored the flat stink of dung that someone hadn't cleaned up behind their mount. The dragon's musk clung to the lawn where it had lain—recent, but not new. He shook his head. "I'm just smelling the remnants of earlier."

The smell was stronger at the side of the stable, where Salome had been standing with the racer and his dragon little more than an hour before.

"She could be anywhere by now," he said as he walked the edge of the smell's range, searching for a path of scent leading away. He found none, merely walking a circle around the stable. "She obviously isn't here, but her smell leads nowhere." He slapped his hand to his forehead. "She could have flown. She could be anywhere."

"I thought you said she was too scared to fly."

"Maybe not if something else scares her more."

They circled the stable again. He smelled a blast of horse as a pegasus walked up the driveway, but the dragon's scent trail was not so clear—it seemed the dragon hadn't gone, but it hadn't stayed, either.

He flopped back against the wall of the building. "I've lost her. Even if she flew just a short distance and landed, it's long enough that I won't be able to pick up her trail again. She could have landed five hundred feet, a mile, two miles from here in any direction, and I'd never be able to find her. I'd have to engineer—I don't know—a sniffer bird just to fly about and try to track her down."

"Stop, babe. Let's assume, for now, that she didn't take off and fly. Where could she have gone? She's obviously not outside. Did her trail lead anywhere besides around the stable?"

"No. Where else is there?"

"How about up?"

Travis tilted his head back, the tip of his vision traveling straight up to the top of the building. "You think she climbed up?"

"Awful safe and quiet up there, don't you think?"

"Worth a try," he said, but when they took the elevator up, they found the roof was indeed quiet and empty—very empty.

"There goes that," said Travis. He sat on a short concrete wall. The thrill of his change and the chase had worn away, leaving him heavy again. He stretched on his side on the low wall and pillowed his head on his hands.

"Oh, no," said Salome, patting his thigh. "You're not going to fall asleep on me now."

"Not falling asleep on you," he murmured.

"Har har. Come on." She tweaked his ear, and he jumped up with a yelp. She gave him a sideways look that was entirely feline, then sashayed to the edge of the roof. She placed her hands on the low border wall and looked down. "So, you really want to give up?"

He looked down over the city, with its million twinkling lights. He imagined how far a dragon could get, driven by fear— or frozen in place because of it. It could have gotten anywhere— or nowhere at all. "I don't know," he said at last. "Where would *you* go if everything terrorized you?"

A short laugh. "Under my covers. Remember? I used to be so scared of closet monsters. I'd spend all night under the blankets."

Travis had always thought it odd that Salome slept with her head under the blanket. It must have been a habit carried on from childhood. He couldn't stand the stifling warmth, himself.

"Travis," said Salome, voice small and distant as she hung her head over the side of the building. "Did you know that the aerie door was open?"

He joined her and looked down. "I noticed *an* aerie door open. Was it mine?"

"Number 39?"

"Yeah. Oh." He'd been in such a rush chasing the dragon he'd forgotten it. Light dawned. "There is one place we haven't checked."

They looked at each other. Together, they said, "Inside."

When he opened the door to the aerie, a rush of dragon smell washed over him.

"Yeah?" asked Salome as Travis sprang into the room. He only remembered stealth and tact as he nearly burst into the stall. The dragon, curled in the far corner under a fringe of straw, looked up and immediately turned into a loose pile of hay.

"Dammit!" Travis clutched the doorway of the stall, every muscle freezing.

Salome let out an appreciative whistle. "Neat trick. Nice mod."

"No no no," Travis said when the haystack undulated, as if the dragon prepared to flee. He took a calming breath and restrained himself from pouncing onto it. In a carefully controlled voice, he said, "Dragon. Hold on." He reached slowly into the pocket of his pants and pulled forth a salmon cube. The dragon's eyes appeared as if peering through the hay, and then the straw around its eyes melted into smooth skin again. "There you are," encouraged Travis. "Let's see your beautiful face."

But the dragon must have remembered Travis's past deceptions using salmon cubes as bait, for it stopped mid-investigation to stare at him suspiciously.

Travis gritted his teeth. "Salome," he said softly, without moving. "Reach into my back pocket—slowly—and pull out the hypo."

"You brought a needle?" she asked.

"In case she wouldn't take the cube. I mixed the virus solution with a bit of tranquilizer."

"Smart," she murmured.

He felt her fingers tugging gently at the lip of his back pocket and slipping the syringe out. "Careful," he warned, as the dragon's gaze flicked to Salome. He held his hand at waist level, fingers facing backwards, palm up. Salome pressed the syringe to his palm. He closed his fingers around it and felt a small tug as she uncapped it for him. "Thanks," he muttered.

The movement of his arm as he readied the needle caught the dragon's attention. With a strange throaty whimper, it heaved to its feet. The sound of its movement crashed in Travis's ears. He sprang forward, narrowly missing a wing as the dragon snapped it open. He struggled, sought flesh, nearly dropped the syringe—plunged.

The dragon dropped to the ground.

Travis collapsed bonelessly atop his mount. When he opened his eyes, he found Salome looking down at the two of them, amusement in the arch of her eyebrow.

"Surprise," she sing-songed, softly. She smiled. "And that was just for *your* birthday. I wonder what you'll do for *mine?*"

When **Christine Danse** isn't studying for her graduate degree in nursing, she likes to write about biopunk. And steampunk. And paranormal romance. And dragons, shapeshifters, gargoyles, alchemy, spirits, trees, children of gods, demons, and—yeah—the *occasional* vampire. But she likes sexy zombies better.

Her first novella, *Island of Icarus*, was released in 2010 by Carina Press. She maintains a steampunk-themed home page, a Muse-friendly Tumblr blog, and a Smashwords site where she occassionally uploads free short ebooks. She also blogs regularly at The Biopunk Reader, her genetically-altered blog baby.

She lives in Florida with her best friend, a camera-shy dog, and two vocal cats. Home page: www.christinedanse.com

Dr. Circe and the Separatist Man-Cheetahs
Erik Scott de Bie

> Mere goodness can achieve little against the
> power of nature.
>
> Hegel

They came over the hills at the darkest hour of the night, loping through the tall grass like moonshadows beneath a starless sky. They ran on the curved legs of cheetahs.

They ran in a pack—half a dozen sleek forms flying across the craggy plain. Weapons glittered, as did claws and fangs. As they ran, the creatures of the field fled around them, sheltering in their holes and caves beneath the waving grasses.

They crossed the border into the land once called Utah when the watchers on the guard towers could not see, bounding high over the barbed fence. One after another, they leaped, sailed through the air, and landed running on the other side.

They ran, intent on the tower in the distance—intent on their mission.

The black clinic in the isolated Utah badlands didn't look as forbidding as he'd expected. Internet speculation and the stories told by regulars in the country diners along the drive held that the tower rose from the broken ground like a spike into the sky, surrounded perpetually by a writhing black storm and wheeling lightning like something out of a bad Frankenstein movie. Local legends held that giant monsters roved the place, some towering hundreds of feet in the air and breathing fire.

An appropriate laboratory for Dr. Circe, the Bio-Witch of the South.

In reality, it looked much like any other desert military bunker fallen out of use since the American Dissolution. It was three stories of stucco reinforced with iron bars, overgrown with vines, and surrounded with razor-wire fence. If not for his GPS, he'd never have found the ruin.

The instructions said to wait, so wait he did. Ulysses turned the engine off.

At the gate, he was sure he'd made a mistake. These were the coordinates, all right, according to the GPS. But the comm.-box looked like a battered tissue box with wires poking out. A yellow flower on a curling green vine protruded from the broken device.

He heard a chirp. He leaned out, thinking that maybe the comm.-box was talking to him anyway. The flower growing from it flourished wide in the light.

"Uh, I'm Ulysses S. Bradbury," he said to the flower-box. "The inspector?"

No reply, naturally. The box was dead as history. The flower, however—he felt like it was watching him, like an old portrait where the eyes seem to move. When he tested it, sure enough, the flower moved with him. OK, *that,* Ulysses thought, was weird.

It got even weirder when a ground squirrel hopped up on the windowsill of his SUV and started talking. "Howdy," it said in a woman's voice. "Password, please."

"Gah!" Ulysses pressed himself back in his seat.

"Don't worry, ah don't use rabid animals." The squirrel cocked its head to the side. "Password, if y'all don't mind."

Ulysses recovered himself enough to get over the weirdness of talking to a squirrel. Which was a considerable exertion of willpower, if he didn't say so himself. "Helios," he said.

The squirrel sniffed the air. "You're new," it said. "What happened to Bob?"

"He's sick," Ulysses said. "Acute liver failure."

"Guess that's goin' 'round."

There was a buzz, and the gate swung open. The squirrel scampered away. The flower on the comm.-box seemed to give him a welcoming smile.

"Now that's just unsettling," Ulysses murmured.

From the backseat, a sickly stench was starting to creep up. He turned the fan up.

The facility looked even more run-down inside the fence than outside, but now that Ulysses had seen the smiling flower and the talking squirrel, suddenly it held menace. The cheery rose bush by the entrance, for instance, might sprout legs and come after him. Every one of the trees potentially had claws, and guard beasts might lurk in the high grass.

He felt under his left arm for the familiar weight of his pistol. Check.

"Nothing for it," Ulysses murmured. "Our Father defend us."

He went inside the old bunker, and the door sealed itself behind him.

Half-man, half-beast, the man-cheetahs watched the SUV drive into the compound, but couldn't make the run before the gate closed behind it. Their commander—the Alpha—stopped them with a gesture, and they circled around, stalking low with their feline posture.

Instead, they gathered outside the compound, lurking in the shadows. Their cat-like eyes gleamed—pupils like slits drew in the light and scanned the fenced complex.

They growled and waited.

Ulysses passed through a gleaming airlock, which blasted him with air so humid he broke into a light sweat. Mechanisms whirred, and the inner door clicked open.

The interior was a vast, flourishing garden, with tropical trees, fountains, and row upon row of plants. The place was open, airy, and positively glowing: someone had opened up ten or so skylight windows in the roof. Even as he watched, the glass shifted alignment to focus the sunlight in different spots to moderate temperature. A greenhouse in an army depot.

Ulysses, who hadn't seen anything like this in years, stood staring. "Wow," he said.

"Well, howdy there," a woman drawled behind him.

Again, the woman who came swaying awkwardly through the foliage defied expectations. He'd been prepared for a harried, frizzy woman with thick glasses—a female mad scientist, possibly—not the slim strawberry-blonde in a lab coat over a white-and-red flowered dress and white stockings. Her hands and knees were dirty, and she had a spade in one hand.

"You must be the new inspector," she said. "'Bout time—ah been waiting all darn day!"

"Ulysses Bradbury," he said. "Are you—are you Doctor Circe?"

"That's what ah'm called in certain less-than-professional circles," she said in her lazy accent. "Callie-Anne Ceres, pleased to make your acquaintance." She put out her hand.

He took her hand and had the sudden urge to kiss it. Her whole demeanor was like something out of *Gone with the Wind*.

"Ah do believe you're staring." She smiled shyly.

"You're—you're not what I expected."

"How so?" Circe looked genuinely intrigued.

Ulysses thought of what he'd read about her: the great geneticist Dr. Circe, who'd built all those weapons for the New Confederates. She specialized in biowarfare, and not the kind with bombs that killed thousands—that was just her hobby. Mainly, she spliced animal and human DNA to engineer super-soldiers: monsters that lived for ripping and tearing.

The petite southern belle standing there barefoot in her flowered dress didn't match that.

"Can ah ask you something?" Circe wasn't looking at him, but rather up at the ceiling.

He eased his hand out of his coat. "Shoot."

A bead of sweat trickled over her brow. "Ah have this terrible itch on mah backside, but ah can't just scratch with you watching without being impolite sumfin' terrible."

"By all means," Ulysses said.

"Thank you kindly." She raised up her skirt a little, revealing a lacy garter that held up her stocking, and scratched. Her sigh was audible and her relief palpable. "Oh, *mercy.*"

Also, he noted her leg's waxy sheen, which her stocking had hidden. "Prosthetics?"

Circe adjusted the clasp on her left leg, which had come a little loose. "Made 'em mahself," she said. "After the Second Great War of Southern Independence."

"Oh." He made the connection. He'd read that Dr. Circe was handicapped from the war, but he hadn't imagined something quite on this scale. "I'm so sorry."

Circe shrugged. "Long time back." She felt at the hem of her flowery dress, smudging the fabric with her dirty fingers. "Ain't nothing to be sorry for."

A shiver passed through him at those words, and he abruptly remembered why he'd come here. Sweet as she might seem, she was dangerous.

Then she laughed and put her hands on her hips. "Well now, where's mah manners? The humidity in here is outside the optimal human range, so you must be sweatin' like a pig. Which is a'course what you'd call ironic, owing as pigs have ineffective sweat glands."

"Huh?" Ulysses had been distracted by her easy charm and unexpected good looks.

"Sweating like a pig," she continued, unabated. "It actually comes from the smelting process, when you pour iron into the runners and it looks like a sow and piglets and—y'all want some lemonade? Ah grow them all mahself—the lemons, ah mean."

"What?" The abrupt reversal of topic startled Ulysses, and all capacity for articulation left him. God the Father, this was going badly. She was going to see right through him.

"I'll just go get it."

"No, that's—" Before Ulysses could finish, she was off, swaying back across the verdant mounds toward another door that led deeper into the complex. "Wait—"

As though that single syllable stopped her, she wobbled to a halt. She turned her head, a finger on her lips as though shushing herself. Her expression was sly.

"Well, ain't that a wonder," she said. "And here ah was, about to break our contract."

"The contract," Ulysses said. Stop acting like an idiot! "Right."

"And as the contract states," Circe said. "That while you're in the complex, we're to keep in constant contact, for issues of liability an' protection."

"Yours or mine?"

"Both, ah s'pose. Can't rightly nerve gas you while we're in the same room now can ah?" She tapped her lower lip. "Unless I coded it for your DNA. Or coded to ignore mine. Huh."

Ulysses forced an awkward smile. "You don't seem like the type."

"Well, a'course not!" she said brightly. "Unless ah've gone insane or sumfin, which is, a'course, what y'all are here for to inspect. Make sure ah ain't lost all mah marbles and got it in mah head to release a lethal bio-toxin on the northern hemisphere, right?"

"Er, right." She said that with such down-home southern charm that it sounded positively casual. What *had* he volunteered for? "It's just me, incidentally."

"Pardon?" She raised one red-blonde eyebrow.

"Just me," Ulysses said. "You said y'all, but it's just me."

"Right, a'course. Silly me."

Something moved then, in the shadow of the waterfall, and instinct took over. He stepped forward, grabbed her wrist, and reached for his gun in one smooth motion.

"Well, ah never!" Circe said. "Bit jumpy, ain'tcha?"

Whatever it had been, it slinked back into the shadow of the overhanging roots.

"What—what was that?"

He hadn't seen it clearly—just glimpsed rustling tentacles and four beady red eyes.

"Oh, that's just Cuddles," she said. "Pay her no mind."

"Cuddles?"

"Cu-Tl-S, Copper-Thalium-Sulfur based hybrid," she said. "Experiment ah did after the war. Don't worry, she's harmless. Mostly." She looked at his hand on her wrist. "Um."

"Sorry." He withdrew his hand and pushed his hair back out of his eyes. "Sorry about that, ma'am—Doctor. Marine training."

"All right then." Circe rubbed her wrist. "Come along now—ah'll show you the labs."

He followed her, picking his way carefully among the bushes and taking care not to step on any of the flowers. He watched for the thing she'd called "Cuddles," but there was no sign.

One of the man-cheetahs approached Alpha, hackles raised. Black spots shone on his furry skin. "What's taking so long?" he asked. "It hurts. God the Father, it hurts so *bad*—"

With one clawed fist, Alpha swiped him across the nose. The challenger fell back, squealing. He reached for his sidearm, but a M16 muzzle appeared in his face, and he relaxed.

"Do not take the Lord's name in vain." Alpha checked his watch. "We go soon."

They climbed down into narrow tunnels that would have done any bomb shelter proud. Sealed by reflective metal doors, every room seemed like its own botanical garden, with flowers ranging from the pedestrian to the exotic to the bizarre.

"Lots of, um, plants in here," Ulysses observed as they walked.

"Mostly mold actually," Dr. Circe said as she swayed on. Her prosthetics gave her a funny, awkward way of walking. "Staple of biochemistry."

She opened one of the rooms with a keycard she wore around her neck. Inside stood shelves with plants encased in glass and numerous Petri dishes. She opened one of the jars.

"Fleming may have discovered Penicillin only a hundred years ago, but folks been treating suppurating wounds with mold since the Middle Ages. Here, wanna try?"

"A suppurating wound?"

"Nah, silly." Circe dipped a spoon into a dish of orange-and-pink mold. "All your daily nutrients in this one little taste. Tastes like sweet potatoes."

"Er, I'll pass."

"Suit y'own self." Circe put the spoon between her lips and sighed blissfully. "Just like Momma used to make."

She looked so happy with her creation that Ulysses felt pleased by extension. Her good will was infectious. "Shall we continue?" he asked.

"Let's." She wobbled as she turned.

"Here"—Ulysses offered his arm—"let me help you."

Circe pulled up short and looked at him fiercely. "Ah appreciate the gesture, but ah've no need for such help," she said. "Ah've lived here on my own quite a while—just me and Cuddles, and he don't talk much. But the point is ah can walk by mah own self, thank y'all very much."

"Consider it a gentleman's offer."

"Well now, when you put it *that* way." She took his arm. "Ah accept."

They strolled from the room like a courting couple.

Down the hall, a colony of pigs grumbled and shuffled behind one of the glass doors.

"Pigs and humans have a high percentage of similarity in their DNA, equivalent or higher—depending on who you ask—than that of humans and chimps," Circe said. "'Sides, a lady can only eat vegetarian so long before she's gotta do some barbecue, y'know?"

They came to a room with CCTV monitors, and Ulysses realized it was the control room. Circe keycarded the door open, and a cacophony of bird chirping, wind whistling, and other sounds assailed them. It was almost like they'd stepped through the door into the outside world.

"Sorry 'bout that." Circe let go of his arm and stepped forward. She hit MUTE, and abruptly the sounds cut off.

"Wow." He hadn't seen much surveillance outside, but from the looks of that room, Circe had every inch of the complex covered. Some of the cameras even *moved*—not side to side, like conventional CCTVs, but like someone was carrying it. "Squirrel cams?" he suggested.

"Nah," Circe said. "Some of them are flowers, and a few are crows."

"Crows?" Sure enough, one of the "cameras" took off and soared up into the sky.

"Bird's ah-view," she said. "It's not that hard, splicing fiber optics into organic DNA. Well, ah s'pose it helps if you have four degrees from M.I.T."

"I guess it would."

He realized she was looking at him very directly—suspiciously? He turned from the monitors and gave her that smile that always seemed to work on the ladies. "What?"

"What d'you think of what ah do here?" she asked carefully.

"I—" He smiled. "I'm not contracted to have an opinion."

She returned his smile. "Friendly question."

"I think it's fascinating," he said. "Your work is a true wonder of the era."

"Believer, eh?" Then Circe added, warily: "Y'all got religion?"

"Not like the Evas, if that's what you mean."

"It ain't," Circe replied. "Just mighty funny, religious man in a black clinic."

He shrugged. "Some of us believe God made humans perfect, no changes needed. Some, like myself, think He meant us to use the minds He's given us to perfect ourselves."

"Reckon that makes sense," Circe said. "Me, I try to steer clear of any God or Goddess, if y'all don't mind."

"Not at all." Ulysses paused a moment. "Sorry if I offended you."

"Nah, nah," she said. "Lost both mah parents in the flood in Nawlins, when ah was away at school. Ain't never been back, after that."

Ulysses felt a little sting of remorse. "I'm so sorry. I didn't mean—"

"Wow, look at that time." She checked her watch. "Reckon y'all interested in the vault."

Ulysses's heart beat faster, but he tried to keep any sign off his face. "Is that were you keep the CBD?"

Circe looked at him quizzically. "Why so interested?"

Immediately, Ulysses back-pedaled. "I'm not," he said.

"Then y'all won't mind if we get some lemonade," she said. "Walking around so much ain't as easy for me, y'know."

"Sure," he said, disappointed at the delay. "That sounds great."

As they went, he lingered half-a-step at the control panel. He flicked a switch. There was no sound, of course, since she'd hit MUTE. On the far right monitor, a light flashed and the gate he'd come in slid open. Sleek forms flitted through.

"Well come on, now," Circe called from the hallway. "That lemonade don't drink itself."

The gate opened, just as Commander Alpha had said it would.

"For God and the New Confederacy," he said.

The other man-cheetahs nodded. Weapons at the ready, the six of them stormed into the facility, paws beating at the grass.

They had lemonade in Circe's quarters—a small, humble chamber that housed her cot and a few personal effects. She used framed college degrees as coasters, which Ulysses found odd but Circe didn't seem the least concerned over.

Ulysses was nervous. The time was right. He had to do it now, or she'd head back upstairs, and they'd lose their window of opportunity.

"What's the matter, sugah?" Circe asked. "Nah, let me guess."

"Sure." He smiled ingratiatingly.

"Ah reckon," Circe said, "y'all taken to wondering why ah ain't made something better."

"Better?"

"For mah legs, I mean."

"Oh." Ulysses indicated her false legs. "Well yeah. I mean, if you can grow a new pair, or splice on a pair of legs from . . . I don't know, a gazelle, or a *cheetah*, why wouldn't you?"

He realized what he'd said too late.

"Cheetah," Circe said. "You know, funny story about—oh."

Ulysses reached across the table and stopped her lips with a kiss. Circe's whole body went taut, and whatever she'd been about to say vanished into the ether.

It ended, and they gazed into each other's eyes for a moment. Then she looked away.

"Sorry," Ulysses said, suddenly self-conscious. "I didn't mean—"

"It's all right," she said. "Ah just—ah'm not used to it, y'know?"

She put her hand on the table, and he took it in his own. This seemed to calm her, for which he prayed thankfully. He only had to keep her distracted a bit longer . . .

"Reckon you know where your name comes from? Circe?"

"No—ah mean, sure, but ah'd like you to say it."

Ulysses smiled. "Circe was a witch in the *Odyssey*, who dwelt all alone in an island castle, patrolled by the beasts of the field and forest," he said. "After Troy fell, when Odysseus came to the island, Circe fed his men magic potions that turned them into animals. The clever captain saw through her tricks, and—made immune by the gods' own magic—he won free."

"Ah do believe you're forgettin' sommat," Circe said. "After he had defeated the witch, he courted her and spent a year in her pleasurable company." She looked at him demurely. "That why you kissed me then?"

He smiled. "Well—"

"You're a Confederate man, right?" Circe asked.

Ulysses paused. That, he had not expected. "Why do you ask?"

"Your accent's mostly gone, but ah can hear traces—you

knew to correct me when I said y'all," she said. "When I axed permission to scratch mahself, you didn't blink an eye. And you knew just the right offer to make about giving me your arm." She looked at him very directly. "You're a southern gentleman, ah do believe."

"So maybe I am," he said. "What of it?"

"Well, if y'all are lyin' about something that easy, what else you lyin' 'bout?" she asked. "Your name, I reckon? Ulysses—the Roman name for Odysseus. Y'all are pretty obvious."

"You keep saying y'all." He reached into his coat.

"Well there's more than one'f you, ain't there?"

That was when the lights went off, replaced by flashing red lamps in the ceiling and corridor. An alarm sounded: "Perimeter Breach," it said in Circe's voice. "Intruder Alert."

"So that's why you kissed me just then—when you mentioned cheetahs," she said. "That was y'all, wasn't it?"

"Not me." Ulysses drew his pistol and put it to her chin. "It's my brother. He's—"

"One of mine," Circe said. "Yeah, ah kinda figured."

"He was ok for a while, but since the war, he's been falling apart," Ulysses said. "I—I have to do what he says. If you do what he wants, it'll work better for everyone."

"Ah'm not the sort to back down from beatings ah've earned, nor run from mah sins when they come a'knockin'. " Circe looked at him with a weary expression. "Well, y'all are the one with the gun. What d'we do now?"

"There's a good mad scientist." Ulysses indicated her exposed leg with his pistol. "Don't take those off yet, doctor. I'll need you to walk." He waved to the corridor. "Now, please."

Circe blew out a sigh. "I was afraid of this. I really had hopes for you, sugah."

"I don't mean for you to get hurt," Ulysses said. "You've been nice to me. Real nice." He cocked his pistol. "But I will put a bullet in your pretty little face if you don't do as I say."

"Well that's very nice a'you, to call me pretty an' all." With composure, Circe rose and dusted herself off. "Half a woman such as mahself gets few compliments as it is."

He led her down the hall, to the storage closet he'd seen

on the way in. He gestured her inside, and she went without a fuss.

"One question," she asked. "Out of curiosity—you really like me, or was it all play?"

Ulysses didn't answer that. "You knew from the start, didn't you?"

"Mah crows picked y'all up three days back—half-man, half-cheetahs stand out a bit."

"So why'd you let me in?" Ulysses asked.

"Ah was just lonely," she said. "Ain't seen nobody but Bob for goin' on five years now. Y'all was a sight for sore eyes, and I thought you was cute an' all."

Ulysses smiled awkwardly. "Thanks," he said. "I wish it was different, but—"

"Ah understand," she said. "Tell yer brother I'm sorry—ah can't do nuthin' for him."

"What?" Ulysses felt cold. "But you're Dr. Circe. You work *magic.*"

"It's just chemistry." Circe looked sad. "Ah can't really fix something after it's been born. Why d'you think I gave up rebuilding people in the war? The more I try, the more unstable they get. I really can't do anything for your brother."

For a long time, they stood face-to-face, him out in the corridor, her in the closet. The alarm blared, and they could hear pounding sounds from above.

"Your legs," Ulysses said.

The color drained from Circe's face. "No," she said. "You don't have to—"

"I'm sorry," he said. "It's awful, but I have to make sure you can't escape."

Circe's face grew angry. "You can at least be a gentleman and turn around."

He shook his head. "I'm very sorry."

Her lip trembling, Circe raised her skirt. She undid the clasps that held the prosthetics to her stumps. With each one, she made a little noise that was half-sigh, half-whimper.

"Help me, why don't you?" she asked, her earlier charm vanished.

He lifted her free of the legs, and set her on the floor. The muscles of her arm flexed taut as she balanced herself against the walls and shelf. She crossed her arms and glared at him.

He nodded, took her legs and locked her in the closet.

The others arrived moments later, loping through the front door into the arboretum. Having disabled the security system, Ulysses went to meet them, pistol in hand.

The big alpha man-cheetah came through the airlock first, and he broke the mechanism to hold it open for the others. The humidity rushed out, diffusing into the arid Utah afternoon. The man-cheetahs loped in, M16s scanning each direction, Kevlar creaking over their furry hides. They stalked low, powerful feline legs ready to spring.

"Watch for her creature," Ulysses warned. "It's some kind of hybrid thing with multiples eyes and tentacles. I think it's hiding somewhere in here. She calls it Cuddles."

Alpha—Ulysses' brother—gave hand-signals to his soldiers, and they fanned out, searching the arboretum. Their heavy boots tramped through flowers and muddied the exotic grasses. This stirred an unhappy ache in Ulysses' chest, though he couldn't say why.

"Have you got her?" Alpha asked. "The doctor who did this to us?"

"Locked in a closet downstairs," Ulysses said. "But she's useless. She said she can't fix you." He shook his head. "I don't think she was lying."

That assertion met whines from the man-cheetahs, but Alpha wore a stoic expression. "Get her to talk," he said. He motioned two of his soldiers down below, and they bounded off, anticipatory smiles on their faces. Ulysses' skin crawled.

"And besides, the bio-witch isn't the prime objective. We're here to carry on the glorious war." Alpha stepped closer to Ulysses. "Where are the CBD canisters?"

"Brother," Ulysses said. "I did this to get you fixed, and if she can't—"

Alpha smacked Ulysses across the face. He fell, and hot

lines of pain bloomed. He felt at the blood Alpha's claws had drawn.

Alpha growled: a sound half-purr, half-pant. There was little of humanity in Alpha's cat-like eyes or furry face—more of the great cat Circe had spliced into him. "CBD," he said.

Agent Charybdis was why they'd come: the last bio-weapon Circe engineered before the events that had led to her leaving the war—and taking her research with her. No one was quite sure what it did, but stories told by embittered veterans held that it could kill every living thing in a mile radius, excepting whatever specific DNA code its handlers programmed in. If the Confederates'd had something even half that effective, they'd have won, and the American Dissolution would have followed a very different path. It might again, if Alpha had his way.

"I didn't see them on my tour," Ulysses said, "but we didn't get to the vault."

"Did you get her to unlock it?"

"No. The alarm went off before I could." Ulysses saw anger grow on his brother's face and knew fear. "But we should be able to open it from the control room."

"Fine," Alpha said. "What is it?"

"I—we don't have to hurt her, do we? Dr. Circe? Just take what we want and go?"

Alpha's expression turned sour. "She got to you, did she? That bitch."

"No, it isn't like that." Ulysses said the words, but he wasn't sure they were true.

"Because of her," Alpha said. "I'm in constant pain. My body fights against itself. She dies tonight, and all our oppressors from the North shortly thereafter."

"But—"

"Shut up, or you can die too." The radio at Alpha's ear buzzed, and he touched it. "Say again? You can't *find* her?" He looked to Ulysses. "Which closet did you say?"

"There's only the one," Ulysses said. "She doesn't have legs. How could she—?"

A dozen flowers about the arboretum suddenly swelled and buzzed with static. "Is this durned thing on?" came Circe's voice.

Alpha looked at Ulysses, totally confused.

"Howdy," Circe said through the flowers. "It's so nice of y'all to stop by, but if y'all would kindly vacate the premises, ah'd be much obliged."

"Control room," Alpha said. "Lead me—"

A terrified yowl cut between them, and gunfire rang out in a thunderous arc. There, beneath the waterfall, one of the Kevlar-wearing man-cheetahs struggled in the grasp of a horrific creature from beyond Ulysses's nightmares. It had six heads, each of them with four gleaming red eyes and snapping jaws, and from its waist protruded tentacles with canine fangs that dripped venom onto the grass. The man-cheetahs sprayed it with their M16s, to little effect.

"Reckon y'all have met Cuddles by now," Circe said. "Ah'd go, if ah were you."

"Go!" Alpha cried, drawing a bead with his assault rifle. "Get to the control room! Now!"

Ulysses ran for the hatch as the man-cheetahs attacked the many-headed, many-armed creature. They fired their guns and leaped from rock to rock, dodging its attacks with feline grace. As he watched, one of them stumbled and ended up in the creature's jaws. It whined and screamed, and Cuddles bit it in half.

"Containment Initiated," the alarm said in Circe's voice. She sounded remarkably upbeat about it.

The hatch slid closed, and Ulysses barely made it inside before it clamped shut and locks swung into place. Gleaming red from the flashing alarm, the tunnel took on a menacing character, as though he were climbing through Hell. He stumbled toward the control room.

"Containment Complete," said the alarm. "Purge Initiated."

"Purge?" Ulysses couldn't hear himself in the blaring alarm.

Through the glass on the lab doors, he could see sprinklers spraying some sort of sticky gray substance on the plants. At first, he didn't understand, but then sparks flew in the rooms, and suddenly all was engulfed in flame. He staggered back from the nearest door with a cry.

"Lab Zero-Eight," the voice continued, "Unsealed."

Ulysses heard a hiss and saw the clamps on one of the doors swivel open. The door swung ajar, and a horde of pigs rushed out, filling the corridor. He drew his pistol, but even in doing so he knew he couldn't get more than a few shots off before they trampled him. Instead, he saw a low-hanging pipe and jumped for it. The pigs raced under him as he held himself aloft. They ran as far as they could from the heat of the various doors and burrowed into the walls, wallowing in the cool earth.

"Ineffective sweat glands," he remembered Circe saying

He made it to the control room, where he saw Circe sitting in the big swiveling control chair. She looked completely at ease as she surveyed the monitors filled with battle and occasionally reached out to press flashing red buttons.

"Open the door!" Ulysses tapped his pistol on the window, drawing her attention. Circe looked over at him, shrugged, and went back to her work.

"Open the—God dammit!" He stepped back, leveled his pistol at the window, and fired.

The glass spider-webbed but didn't break. The bullet ricocheted off the window, hit the floor, and blasted into his thigh with a searing pain. Ulysses cried out and fell to the floor, grasping at the welling blood. He'd nicked an artery, he thought.

As he lay there, staring at the pigs down the hall trying to burrow out, his senses shattered by the blaring alarm, Ulysses thought maybe he'd made some missteps in his life.

The door to the control room whined as the locks disengaged, and it opened of its own accord. Dr. Circe peered out at him from the control seat.

"Ooh, that looks terrible," she said. "Y'all pardon me if I don't get up."

Legless, she turned back to the monitors and clicked more buttons. Down near the floor, he saw the opening to a narrow tunnel and realized she must have crawled from the closet. She had expected all of this, he realized.

Ulysses grunted upright, clenched his leg hard in one

hand, and hobbled into the control room. He pointed the gun at Circe. "Call it off . . . now!"

"It's hardly mah fault your brother's gone and made Cuddles lose her religion," she said without looking. "Though when ah told you about her a'first, I might have left out a few details."

"Like how she's a monster?" Ulysses suggested.

"Most awful thing ah could imagine," she said. "Ah named her Scylla a'first—thought y'all might appreciate that, being all mythological and such."

The monitors showed her multi-limbed monster tearing apart the man-cheetahs, seemingly heedless of their bullets.

"Call it off'—Ulysses pulled the hammer back with his teeth—"or I shoot you right now."

"Oh please." Circe gave him a dubious look. "You need me to treat that there bleeding leg wound, or y'all won't last two minutes."

"That's my brother up there," Ulysses said. "You're just going to let him die?"

"An' mah alternative is to let him get what he wants, and kill millions with Charybdis?" she asked. "What kinda dumb-ass question is that?" She turned back to the monitors. "Better that six men die than sixty million. Or do you not agree?"

He put the gun to her head. "Call it off," he said. *"Now."*

She looked at him very seriously. "You might want to reconsider shooting me," she said. "Or at least do it quick-like."

"Why?" he asked.

" 'Afore ah press this." She touched a red button, and the monitors suddenly started flashing a warning message.

"Charybdis Initiated," the alarm said cheerily. "T-minus ninety seconds to reach minimum safe distance of one mile."

"What's that?" he asked.

"Self destruct sequence," Circe said. "You think ah picked this spot in Utah by accident? It has certain geologic properties that amplify the CBD, and it's far from civilization. When that timer runs down, this whole place will sink into the ground like it never existed."

"But why would you do that?" he asked. "You're

winning!"

"The things ah keep in this place… they should never have existed in the first place. Ah see that now." She shook her head. "This is the only way to keep some monster from loosing them on the whole world." She pushed another button, which flashed green. "Ah've opened the door. Let the pigs out on your way—they don't deserve to go down the whirlpool."

"But—" He looked at her bare stumps. "You can't get out of here in that time. You'll die."

She shrugged. "Only a quarter of the evil ah've done is in this place," she said. "But all of it's in mah head. Again, it's a dumb-ass question."

Ulysses paused, stunned. He thought of his angry brother, hungering to kill millions in a war that had ended years ago. He thought of Circe's horrible monster, doing what she had bred it to do. He thought of Circe herself, ready to die to protect the world from herself.

He thought of the pigs with their ineffective sweat glands.

He came to a decision.

The isolated installation in the Utah badlands ceased to exist.

There was no explosion, nor any release of poisonous gas or noxious fumes to melt the buildings. Instead, the earth shivered, and a whirlpool drew the facility down into the ground. It carried the warring man-cheetahs and the hybrid bio-creature down into the maelstrom.

A single black SUV rolled out of the chaos just as the whole thing came crashing down.

Where the bunker had been emerged a flowing expanse of green. The hurricane of earth shifted in shade and texture into leafy tones, and vines spread a mile in every direction. In the center, the seething morass of vegetation boiled up and around itself, building higher and higher until it froze in place. The vines fell away to reveal deep red, living bark.

"A tree," said Ulysses. "So Dr. Circe's last an' greatest bio-weapon was a *tree.*"

Seated beside him in the passenger seat of the SUV, Circe shrugged. "One of the core rules of biochemisty," she said. "Ain't nuthin' stronger than Mother Nature. So don't piss her off."

"No kidding." Ulysses slumped back in the seat and breathed.

They sat together, looking out at the new forest growing in the Utah desert. The colony of pigs in the trunk oinked contentedly.

"Why'd you bring me out of there, anyway?" Circe said. "And don't say ah'm a good kisser, 'cuz ah already know that."

Ulysses blew out a long sigh. He wasn't sure exactly why he had carried her out, put her in his car, and drove off. It had just seemed like the right thing to do.

"I know you don't truck much with God or the good book." He threw the SUV into drive. "But in all this mess, you're the only light, and I'm not in the habit of making things darker."

"Well," she said with a smile. "Always did want to plant more trees.

Quite possibly a bio-engineered monster in disguise (the height is a dead give-away), **Erik Scott de Bie** writes speculative fiction from under an abandoned military compound in Seattle. He takes inspiration from music, movies, and his cats, who form the basis of his genetic experiments. (So far, all that kibble has only produced bigger cats, but he's holding out for more exciting results.)

Primarily a fantasy author, he has published four Forgotten Realms novels: *Ghostwalker, Depths of Madness, Downshadow,* and the forthcoming *Shadowbane* (due out this fall). His work has also appeared in numerous anthologies such as *Beauty Has Her Way, When the Hero Comes Home,* and *Cobalt City Timeslip* from Timid Pirate Publishing.

If his work delights, frustrates, or perhaps just entertains, hunt down Erik on facebook or twitter (under his full name), on his blog (eriksdb.livejournal.com), or at his website (www.erikscottdebie.com), and give him your feedback.

About Timid Pirate

Timid Pirate Publishing is a small, independent, nonprofit publisher determined to seek and share adventures of the highest caliber. Inspired? Delighted? Tell your friends and family and then start drawing or writing, because we always have at least one call for submissions.

Since pirates have booty, visit our website (timidpirate.com) for free PDF downloads of stories and to find our podcast, where stories are given voice.

Previous Publications:

Cobalt City Blues, 2010
Cobalt City Christmas, 2010
Cobalt City Timeslip, 2010

Forthcoming Publications:

Cobalt City: Dark Carnival, 2011